MW01099044

They Sleep
with the
Fishes

THE COSENZA BROTHERS -
THE EARLY YEARS OF ADVENTURE

To Rylee
I hope you
enjoy this
book.

Vaughn L. Paragamian

Merry Christmas
2019

VAUGHN L. PARAGAMIAN

ISBN: 978-1-4834-4283-9 (sc)
ISBN: 978-1-4834-4282-2 (e)

Because of the dynamic nature of the Internet, any web addresses or links contained in this book may have changed since publication and may no longer be valid. The views expressed in this work are solely those of the author and do not necessarily reflect the views of the publisher, and the publisher hereby disclaims any responsibility for them.

Any people depicted in stock imagery provided by Thinkstock are models, and such images are being used for illustrative purposes only. Certain stock imagery © Thinkstock.

Lulu Publishing Services rev. date: 01/08/2016

CONTENTS

PICTURES

PROLOGUE

This work is a compilation of a series of true stories and events, as shared with me by my mother, primarily experienced by her and her family during the Great Depression. Some of the events are first person accounts of my limited interaction with relatives who were purportedly in the Mob. For example I was asked by a cousin at an Italian wedding if I would like to meet his business partner and become an associate working out of a known Mob lounge. I was reminded of the story in the Bible where Christ was offered the world by the Devil. Money, cars, fine clothes and women would be mine if I joined. The stories are stereotypic examples of the tales you hear in Italian family lore. I have also taken writer license to embellish the stories with fictitious or exaggerated characters and events. This book is offered solely for its entertainment and reading enjoyment and any names are purely coincidental.

In the book we follow Vito and Tony Cosenza through the early years of their lives. The death of their pa, Angelo, leaves emptiness in their hearts that does not heal. Their mother Maria is asked, after Angelo's mysterious death to move in with her family, the Pontillos. Rumors of Angelo's exploits are shared by some in the underworld, but not to the Pontillos. Thugs try to extort the family, thinking they are affluent and have thousands of dollars hidden that was left by a job Angelo pulled. The extortion attempt is foiled when a Mob boss comes to the Pontillos' aid. Eventually Antonio Pontillo repays the favor, but it leads to an unplanned road trip for the Cosenza brothers. The brothers eventually go their own way professionally, but stay close. Big Tony is a rising boxing contender while Vito eventually joins a Mob Family as a business associate. However, a vendetta on those responsible for the death of their pa brings them together to bring justice for their family. Read more and learn of the fulfillment of the vendetta and the outcome.

IN MEMORY

This book is dedicated to the memory of my late brother David Mark Gibson: a loving husband, father, uncle and brother. David loved the stories of the old days as told to us by our mother. The Godfather series were among his favorite movies and Luca Brasi his favorite character. He was the proverbial gentle giant and everyone who met him loved his kind nature and his story telling.

CHAPTER 1

Extortion

In the dark of night a large truck side swiped Angelo's coupe. It sounded like two pieces of steel competing for space, making a loud metal on metal scraping sound. On the second swipe the truck forced Angelo off the road and toward a riverbank. As Angelo's car raced downhill he kept pushing his brake pedal, but there was something wrong. Angelo shouted, "The brakes, they're gone!" Within seconds his coupe rolled further downhill, careened off a tree and into the Chicago River. Angelo's head hit the windshield with a thud; the pain was excruciating. Scenes of Angelo's life raced by him: as he thought of his lovely Maria and his two boys. How did he allow himself to get into this predicament? His thoughts were interrupted when he painfully reached to his head and felt blood sliding down his face. Almost instantaneously he could feel the pain in his chest, it felt crushed. It was impossible to breathe. Angelo could barely hear a voice, "Angelo, Angelo get out, get out!" The voice became fainter and fainter and then he felt nothing as the cold river water flooded his coupe.

Five years later

The lights flickered in the Cook County Jail on July 3, 1929, a typical event when a death row inmate was electrocuted. "Looks like they just fried Costello," Sam Rizzo said in a raspy voice. Rizzo's voice and tall thin body were easily recognized throughout the Cook County Jail and the streets of Chicagoland.

The heavy set Ned O'Brien was struggling to put on a clean pair of socks when he said, "Yeah he was a mean bastard. A loser and deserved the chair as far as I'm concerned."

"You could say that about all of us being losers. Once I get out of here I'm going to hit it big," Rizzo said.

"You'll be back here in a year because you're just another screw-up chump," uttered O'Brien.

Rizzo flipped O'Brien the finger and said, "So what the hell are you, Mr. Success? Besides," Rizzo explained, "I got it figured out. You and I are going to be loaded in a couple of months." O'Brien never took Rizzo's schemes seriously, yet he knew they were desperate. Both would be broke and sleeping in the alleys of Chicago, Waukegan or some shit hole town if they didn't get into some bread money soon after their release. O'Brien could stay with his brother Tom for a short time, but then what? The truth was they were both losers with reputations for thinking they had things figured out and that everyone else was dimwitted. Both were in Cook County Jail for trying to steal a truck five years earlier owned by a smalltime gangster. They had a failed plan for that too and were just lucky Chicago cops caught them with it before the thug did. Neither had a chance of getting a job locally--even cleaning toilets in the cheapest club in Chicagoland was beyond their skill level.

"Lights out," shouted the night corrections officer. A low-level chatter buzzed immediately through the dark.

Picture 1. Cook County Jail in the 1920s. Neighbors of the Cook County Jail usually knew when an inmate was electrocuted because their house lights would flicker. Photo courtesy of the Cook County Sherriff's Office.

"Okay, okay so what's the story on this guy," asked O'Brien.

Rizzo quickly answered, "This is the deal. This old guy by the name of Antonio Pontillo in Kenosha is supposed to be loaded. He works for the railroad, but he's got to have something going on. I was in Kenosha five years ago and this ex-con in Demark's Bar tells me there is a rumor that this Pontillo has thousands stashed in his house. He told me his son-in-law supposedly gave him a load of dough from fenced jewels before he died. We got plenty of angles to get it out of him and if they don't work, he's got a couple grandkids we could nab and hold for ransom."

O'Brien scratched the back of his head, a nervous twitch he had when he was anxious. "You're so full of crap Rizzo; you'd believe anything a drunk told you. Besides it was a rumor."

"Look," rasped Rizzo, "I get out before you do. When you get sprung on July 27, I'll meet you in front of the Carlton at 9 p.m. and I'll lay out the whole plan then. By that time I'll have had a chance to check out his neighborhood. I think Pontillo will be a push-over and we'll score before we have to nab one of his grandkids. It'll be a breeze. He'll give us what we ask for before we have to grab a kid and I think he'll keep his mouth shut. He'll never go to the cops. Cops don't give a shit about any Guinea and especially those that can't speak good old American."

O'Brien gazed at Rizzo as he was taken by the idea. "That's what I like about you Rizzo. You always got things figured out. I don't think you know Jack Shit about Pontillo, but I'll bite because I don't have shit myself. But if this *Goombah* has friends we're sleeping with the fishes and I'll kill you if that happens."

Carmine "The Weasel" Francisco, an inmate in the cell next door, was cupping an ear to hear better and whispered, "Hey Rizzo what's the deal?"

Rizzo had just finished putting his cigarette out when he said, "Screw you Carmine, keep your nose out of this and shut up."

"I get out soon too and I'll be as busted as you guys. I can help."

O'Brien scratched his head and hastily cut in, "No deals. Keep your mouth shut and out of our business. Besides you'll be whacked within a day of getting out of this joint anyway."

Rizzo lay back on his bunk and thought how easy a gig this was going to be, how smart he was, and what he would do with his share of the cash. The dark was again interrupted with Rizzo thinking out loud, "The first thing I'm going to do is get a bottle of booze and find a real woman."

Carmine The Weasel got his nickname because he was a squealer and his sunken cheeks and long nose also gave him the appearance of a weasel. He likely would not see the light of day more than a few weeks after his upcoming release. He had spent a better part of his life in institutions. He was a pipeline of gossip and rumors and seemed to know more about everyone else's business than he should. He just had this way of either listening or drawing information out of people without them really knowing it. It may have been because he just looked so harmless. Sometimes this was a two-edged sword because the cops always needed information and he had gained the disdain of the underworld also.

CHAPTER 2

The Pontillos' Neighborhood

By mid-August Antonio Pontillo had received an anonymous threatening letter. The letter explained he was to put $20,000 in cash in an envelope. At 1:00 a.m. August 30, 1929 he was to place the envelope at the base of a fire hydrant at the south end of his block, and not involve the cops. Failure to comply would result in the Pontillo's home being fire bombed or one of the kids in the house being abducted. After reading the letter a furious Antonio took a deep breath and wondered what fools would write such a letter. Pontillo didn't have $20,000 and at best he had $20. He then summoned his two sons, still living at home, Frank and Roberto. Antonio nervously pulled at his mustache as he explained what was in the letter and that he was not going to give in to extortion. He also said they would devise a plan to protect their home and his two young grandchildren. He didn't believe anyone could really think he had that kind of cash. Later that afternoon, two days after receiving the letter, Antonio visited his neighbor Franco Alvano. He explained to Franco what the letter demanded. Antonio further explained that he couldn't comply, and asked Franco to watch for suspicious characters or anything unusual.

On any given afternoon the Kenosha, Wisconsin neighborhood in which the Pontillos lived was usually busy with chatter, but not this time:

it was very quiet. Normally the chatter was in German or Italian, but seldom English. The neighborhood was ethnically split with German immigrants on the west side of the street and Italians on the east. They were also divided by way of religion, Lutherans on the west and Catholics on the east. Neither side made an effort to learn and speak English because they were comfortable without it. All the people they met at church, stores and close neighbors all spoke their native tongue. The exceptions were the kids who attended public schools: they knew English, but were forbidden to visit the opposite side of the street, which was hard to control.

The neighborhood was strangely quiet because a Waukegan Mob Boss, Al Alvano, had been visiting his brother Franco. Alvano's 1927 Packard was parked out front where his driver waited. None of the German or Italian families wanted to draw attention to themselves. Alvano had a reputation for being intolerant and decisive. Even the cops avoided the block when Alvano was visiting. Two of Alvano's Wise Guys would stand guard, one in front and the other to the rear of the house. While the Alvanos were visiting, Antonio sat on a large porch swing with his two grandsons nearby. Antonio was contemplating the threatening letter and how he would respond if there was trouble.

Al eventually emerged from the house and said out loud, "Antonio, *buonasera paisano.*"

The greeting caught Antonio by surprise. He turned to look and saw Alvano. He took his pipe from his lips and returned the greeting, "*Buonasera.* I'm doing fine Al. You look in good health. Business must be doing you good." Two stark faced Wise Guys stood by. One combed his jet black hair while the other walked to the back door of the Packard and opened it, watching the neighboring homes cautiously. The second, Mean Mike, nodded a greeting to Antonio; he was Antonio's nephew. Al Alvano occasionally visited his brother Franco, who had been Antonio's neighbor for more than twenty years. Franco was older than Al and out of respect and love, Al took time for the occasional visit.

"No, business is driving me crazy." Alvano spread his arms and opened his palms in a questioning gesture. "It's my fine ladies that keep me healthy and happy."

Without taking a breath Antonio asked his oldest grandson, Vito, to go fetch a bottle of *vino* for *Signor* Alvano. Alvano was Vito's Godfather, but was affectionately called Uncle Al by Vito and his younger brother Tony. Vito was off in a flash and moments later delivered the bottle to Alvano. Just as Alvano was rubbing Vito's head Antonio stepped down from his porch and shook Alvano's hand. He liked Alvano as a friend, but not for what he did for a living or what he represented to non-Italians. Alvano was in a felonious profession some Mobsters thought of it as a business of simply providing to the public what they wanted and the government prohibited them from having.

Alvano asked, "Antonio, we have been friends for many years. Is there anything I can do for you and your family?"

Antonio starred down the street at the fire hydrant where the extortion money was to be stashed turned and said, "No we are fine. I would never trouble a friend with anything I can't take care of myself!" Franco had told his brother about the extortion letter Antonio had received.

Alvano held the bottle of *vino* in the air and said, "*Gracia* my dear friend I'll see you again soon. Remember if I can be of help do not be too proud to call on me."

"*Si*, I understand," Antonio said. Despite the fact Antonio was Italian and Alvano Sicilian the two had a deep respect and concern for each other's welfare. Italians in general looked down on Sicilians. Alvano stepped into his car and the door was shut by one of his Wise Guys. The Packard was driven off and the neighborhood chatter gradually picked up.

The trio returned to the porch. Vito glanced up at Antonio, his nanu, with admiration. Since the loss of his pa five years earlier, Antonio had become a father figure. He wondered about Antonio's fearless and adventurous early years and if his would be as adventurous. Antonio was born in 1868 on a farm near Naples, Italy. At the age of 13 Antonio learned how important it was to care for family when he and his father traveled to Argentina for two years to build railroads. Most of their earnings were sent home. At 16, Antonio immigrated to America by himself where he worked in the West laying tracks for the Union Pacific Railroad, and was a deputy sheriff in Wyoming, for a short spell. Antonio had looked the part with a confident swagger, a large handlebar mustache and at 6' 4" and 235 pounds he was intimidating. He returned to Italy and met his wife Giovanna and had his two oldest sons before he returned to Waukegan, Illinois, with his family and to his former job with the railroad. He eventually had four more children. Antonio made sure his four boys had jobs working for the railroad. The fact that all of the adults in the family including his two daughters, Maria and Rose, worked when jobs were scarce gave the appearance of affluence. Neighbors wondered about the Pontillos and possible Mob connections. This wasn't necessarily untrue, as he was friends with Alvano.

After a few moments of daydreaming Vito was distracted by a soft and beautiful voice, "Hi Vito, did you have a nice day?" It was Gwen, the daughter of a German couple who lived across the street.

Vito's heart began to pound as he replied with a smile, "Why yes Gwen. Did you?" Vito had a crush on Gwen and she on him, yet it seemed like they could never carry out a conversation for long without being interrupted. They were an ethnic contrast: Gwen was an attractive blond, fair skin and blue eyes while Vito was average height for his age, black curly hair, dark skin tone and athletic build.

"Are you going to the bike races next Saturday night?" she asked.

"Yes," he answered, wanting to add more. Gwen was immediately summoned by her mom.

Antonio looked at Vito and saw the sparkle in his eyes as Gwen crossed the street. "Vito," said Antonio, "I see you like the young German girl." Antonio paused and said, "Too bad she is not *Italiano* or Catholic." That didn't matter to Vito.

Antonio's two grandsons and their mother Maria had been living with him and Giovanna for several years. Maria was widowed and had moved in at their request after the loss of her husband Angelo Cosenza. It was April 12, 1924 when police delivered the news that her husband was killed in an unusual auto accident in Chicago. His 1923 Chrysler was towed from the crash site and left to rust in a grove of trees near a barn on the Pontillos' four-acre back yard. Maria had been a calm woman until her husband's death, but was devastated after his loss. She was responsible for raising her two boys alone. While Vito was average height, Anthony AKA "Big Tony" got his nickname honestly because at thirteen years of age he was nearly 6 feet tall and about 195 pounds. The boys had been regular kids until their dad's death. They loved their pa and cried night after night for his loss. The added responsibility of working and raising the boys was too much for Maria. Now with the help of family and the counseling of Father Falbo, of Holy Sacrament Church, Maria was getting emotionally stronger. She had become an excellent waitress at Demark's which was only a few blocks from home.

CHAPTER 3

The First Extortion Attempt

The morning of August 30, 1:00 a.m. came quickly. A stolen 1920 Ford Model T pulled alongside a fire hydrant with no letter to be seen. Rizzo got out of the car and searched around the poorly lit hydrant. He quickly jumped back into the sedan and he and O'Brien sped away. "Well smart ass we're still broke. Did you put a damn stamp on your letter?" O'Brien asked.

"Hell I can't remember," responded Rizzo with uncertainty.

"You dumb ass, if you did you probably put my brother's return address on the letter."

"Look I may be forgetful, but I wouldn't do that! I don't even know where he lives."

"Ah bullshit. Now what are we gonna do?" O'Brien asked as he scratched his head driving with one hand.

In a menacing tone Rizzo said, "We'll pay him a visit, we'll pay him a visit tonight. No rough stuff this time, but we'll bust a few windows."

Back at the Pontillo home, Roberto came running into the back yard, leaving Frank in the front to continue watching the street.

"They're serious Pa," whispered Roberto. "We saw their car pull up to the hydrant and speed off."

"What direction?" asked Antonio.

"They drove south," Roberto said.

Antonio then ordered, "Go back to Frank and wait. I think they'll be back and soon. Be careful, they may have guns." Antonio had devised a simple plan. His two boys would stand guard in the front of the house hidden by shrubs and armed with axe handles while Antonio would wait at the back alley with a club and the family dog Rex, a nine year old German shepherd.

Rizzo and O'Brien drove a few minutes trying to work up enough courage to return to the Pontillos' house. The courage was slow to come because they didn't know what to expect. The Pontillos didn't take their letter seriously, but they would not expect a visit. They decided they needed to make a point. Rizzo would be dropped off in the alley at the back of the house and do some damage with a tire iron while O'Brien would smash a few windows in the front. After twenty minutes O'Brien drove slowly through the alley with his lights off and let Rizzo out. He then drove back to 22nd Street and parked on the corner.

Rizzo was nervous as he worked his way through the dark to the back gate. He paused a moment shaking like a leaf. He slowly opened the creaking gate. After a step or two he could hear Rex's low menacing growl. Rizzo shook even more and thought he might piss his pants. Just then Antonio released Rex. Rex grabbed Rizzo's calf muscle and clamped down on it as if the dog was grabbing his last bone. Rizzo howled like a banshee and could be heard for blocks. He swung his tire iron so hard it slipped from his hand, missing Rex. Rizzo tried to run. Antonio commanded Rex to return, "*Ritornare* Rex *ritornare.*" Meanwhile O'Brien had snuck along the very front of the neighboring homes so he would not be seen on the sidewalk. When he came within twenty feet of the Pontillo home, he heard Rizzo scream and he heard Frank tell Roberto to help their pa. O'Brien was ready; Roberto ran the 200 feet to the back. Frank saw O'Brien at the last second as O'Brien came within a few feet of the house. Frank dove at O'Brien's hip and knocked him over. O'Brien quickly recovered and delivered a blow to Frank's side with a two-by-four. The blow made a resounding whump but the second swing missed as Frank folded from the first blow. Frank was just barely capable of swinging his axe handle, striking O'Brien with moderate force. O'Brien's weight was of no consequence as he ran like hell for the sedan that he had left running, jumped in and floored it. A panting O'Brien drove the car recklessly as it swerved around a corner where he picked up Rizzo and high tailed it for his brother's house.

"Pa, you okay?" shouted Roberto.

"*Si* I'm fine and you?"

"*Si*, we need to check on Frank." They found him very sore, but he would be okay.

Antonio then said, "You boys get some sleep. I'll watch for a little while--they won't be back tonight."

"*Si* Pa," Roberto responded. Antonio was proud of his boys, they defended the family and he wanted to make sure they knew they did a good job so he told them so. Just then Maria returned from Demark's exhausted and unaware of what had just happened. She smiled at her pa and two brothers and headed straight to bed unaware of the brawl that had taken place. In the dark Antonio sat back in his wooden lawn chair gradually falling asleep with Rex at his side.

The following morning Antonio cautioned Vito and Tony to go to school and come home only with Frank as a bodyguard. Frank would have the time since he now had a new job at Nash Automotive, a few miles from home.

"Slow down damn it; we got 20 miles to go. You want the cops after us? We got a stolen car here," screamed Rizzo. "And stop scratching your damn head and just drive. I got blood streaming down my leg."

"Screw you Rizzo, they were waiting for us in ambush. You had a dumb ass plan and we could have been killed. I got slammed on the side. What's the blood from?"

"I got bit by their mangy dog; he tore half my leg off," moaned Rizzo.

O'Brien said, "I need a drink and I know where to go to get your leg tended to just don't get me involved in none of this shit again you hear me?"

"Cool it," a more collected Rizzo responded. "I know he's got the money. I know it and we ain't done with this chooch." It was a quiet ride for the next 25 miles. While Rizzo gazed at the occasional house lights he was formulating a new strategy. Neither of the two had ever tried extortion. They were well experienced in petty theft, trying to con fools, they had stolen cars and trucks, and were getting good at rolling drunks before they got canned.

O'Brien turned onto a country road and then to a farm lane that weaved through a woodlot to a farmhouse. To Rizzo's surprise dozens of cars were parked out front. Two thugs approached them as they drove into the lot. "Identify yourselves!" shouted one of the thugs. They were questioned before one recognized O'Brien and said, "Go on in."

Rizzo limped behind O'Brien and a second line of security met them at the door. They walked in and found a small table. Each had a beer and Rizzo's leg was bandaged by an acquaintance of O'Brien's.

A brunette in her thirties walked over to their table and sat down. She had average looks with an exceptional body. As she sat down she asked, "You gonna by me a drink?"

"Yeah sure," said Rizzo.

Then in a sultry voice the brunette asked, "Which one of you wants company for a half an hour?"

"I do," said Rizzo. "How much is it gonna cost besides the drink?"

"How about $50," she responded.

Rizzo choked and spit up beer while trying to say, "How about $5?"

"What the hell do I look like the Salvation Army," she screamed storming away from the table.

"You sure have your way with women," O'Brien said.

Rizzo wiped the beer slobber away from his face. "Well I got my drink, but no woman." Within an hour the two were back on their way to O'Brien's brother's house.

CHAPTER 4

The Second Extortion Attempt

At sunrise Rizzo and O'Brien arrived at a farm house on State Line and were greeted by O'Brien's brother Tom. Tom was a two-bit crook with a part-time job at a warehouse in Waukegan. Tom had been renting the farm house for several months. "So how was the job hunting yesterday?" he asked. Before O'Brien could answer he added, "And who's the skinny *Goombah*?"

O'Brien was caught off guard. "He's a friend, Sam Rizzo and it went well."

"Bull crap." Tom shouted. "He stays a day or two, but rent's the same for him as you. I love you Ned, but I can't afford either of you without something. Now put the car in the barn and out of sight." Tom was renting a cheap and dirty little farmhouse on the outskirts of Kenosha. It was two stories high and owned by a farmer and usually occupied by migratory workers. "Tom, we gotta plan to make some money, I'll explain later," said O'Brien. O'Brien and Rizzo's next plan was to lure the two grandsons from school and grab them to show Antonio how vulnerable he was.

Picture 2. At sunrise Rizzo and O'Brien were greeted by O'Brien's brother Tom, at his rental on State Line.

On Friday morning school officials summoned the Cosenza brothers from their class rooms. "You boys have an emergency at home and we are excusing you to go home immediately," reported the vice principle.

Vito listened intently slowly shaking his head side to side, "No we don't sir. Someone is pulling a prank on our family. We'll stay here till our Uncle Frank picks us up after school."

"Are you sure?" questioned the vice principle.

"Yes I am," Vito said.

"Okay return to your class room." That evening Vito reported the call to his family. That same night Antonio stood guard at the back of his house with an old hand gun and Rex while the Pontillo brothers watched the front with shotguns. Antonio didn't want it to come to this with guns, but he had no doubt these goons would stop at nothing.

Morning broke at the Pontillos as the sun slowly rose from the east. "*Buongiorno* Antonio," whispered Giovanna. "It's time to ready for the market."

Antonio rubbed his eyes and massaged Rex's back and said, "*Si, uno momento.*" Antonio hid his hand gun then grabbed a wooden wagon and pulled it to his garden. With Rex at his side he picked half a bushel of tomatoes, a peck of bell peppers, and a dozen eggplants. Antonio returned to the house, cleaned up, and had breakfast with his wife and grandson Vito. The three of them then headed to the market with the wagon fully loaded and Rex followed behind.

Antonio was distracted all morning with his thoughts of the event two nights earlier and the affair at school. Twice he had given customers the wrong change. "Antonio, Antonio, are you there? That's a dime not a nickel!" scolded Giovanna.

"Oh *excusa* I see!"

"Vito," shouted Giovanna. "Come here and help with change." Vito had exceptional math skills and had dreams of someday working in a bank and doing business deals.

For Antonio the way back home was no different.

"I know what is troubling you Antonio," explained Giovanna.

"I have a more disturbing story besides the letter I told you of and the fight two nights ago," Antonio said. Antonio described in detail all of the events and his renewed concerns for the family. School had started and already there was trouble which added to the situation because his grandsons would sometimes have to walk the mile and a half by themselves. He would need to formulate a plan and then gather the family again to explain assignments. Going to the authorities was completely out of the question for several reasons. Extortion was not uncommon, and to go to the authorities before asking Alvano for help would be an extreme insult. Antonio was a proud man and felt he and his boys could handle these goons. Besides, the cops would consider him an idiot. Local authorities showed little compassion for Italians. They thought they were all corrupt and intertwined with Chicago gangsters which in itself promoted the stereotype that all Italians were criminals. Further there was a continuous effort, sometimes successful, by the Mob to corrupt even the finest cops with payoffs and deals.

Rizzo and O'Brien woke up after spending the night sleeping at Tom's again, neither having slept very well. O'Brien was pissed. "We are totally screwed. I'm broke, I can't stay with my brother much longer, I've got a stolen car in the barn, and I got to cut hanging with a loser like you. None of your plans have worked."

Rizzo came back, "Look we still have a chance of hitting it big. We need one more for my next plan and I think I know who can help."

"Oh shit why do I keep listening to you Rizzo, why do I keep listening to you?" O'Brien grabbed a pack of cigarettes and lit one, puffed on it a couple times and shook his head in futility.

Rizzo walked across the small dining room to Tom, who was sitting at his kitchen table drinking coffee and smoking a cigarette. "Look Tom," said Rizzo in a low tone. "We need your help." Tom looked up at Rizzo with a blank stare.

"What the hell you talking about?" asked Tom. "I got a legit job why would I help you suckers?" Tom got up from his chair turned his back on Rizzo and stared out the front window.

"Look Tom we need you. We tried a little extortion on a guy by the name of Antonio Pontillo. He and his family live in Kenosha. We tried to soak him for twenty grand and it didn't work and yesterday we tried to grab a kid by calling the school to send him home. That didn't work. This time we're gonna figure another plan to nab one of Pontillo's grandkids and hold him for ransom. We need you," whispered Rizzo.

"Holy shit, you gotta be kidding me. You get caught that is life or maybe the chair," said Tom.

"They don't have the chair in Wisconsin," answered Rizzo.

"No, no, dumb ass, but they do in Illinois," answered Tom. "This piece of crap shack is on the Illinois side."

Rizzo started to get nervous. Convincing Tom was not as easy as talking Ned into one of his schemes. "It's a sure thing. After we grab a kid and we get the twenty grand we let him go," answered Rizzo.

Tom was slow to answer. "Give me a couple minutes to think on it. I'm still not as desperate as you two." A couple hours went by as Tom thought of his pointless life. His wife and kids left him, he was barely hanging on to his rental, he had a piece of crap car, he was middle aged, and nothing to look forward too. Hell he couldn't even afford a $2.00 radio. Tom was far shrewder than Rizzo or Ned; he had been in on countless capers and never got caught. If he took over it would be a smoother operation which meant success. "Okay let me in. Let's plan this out, tell me first what's already gone down, and from here I'll do all the planning or no deal," ordered

Tom. "One more thing," Tom said, "we ask for fifty grand—twenty is chump change if he really has what you think he has."

Rizzo rubbed his hands together and smiled while shouting. "Okay, okay you're in and you're the boss."

Sunday morning's preparation for church was as usual for the Pontillos. Everyone woke around six and in succession the washing and bathroom details were done in sequence: women followed by men and then breakfast. Then the family would take the three block walk to Holy Sacrament and sit in the same pew. As the family waited for Mass to begin Vito looked at an exceptionally gorgeous pin worn by his ma. It was shaped like Cupid's bow. "That must be your favorite pin Ma, you wear it a lot," commented Vito.

"It's my favorite," answered Maria. "Your pa gave it to me before he died." Just then Father Falbo entered and walked to the altar and began the Mass.

That Sunday afternoon Antonio brought his family together including his youngest daughter, Rose. In a calm and confident voice Antonio addressed the family. He explained what was in the letter, the fight and what had happened at school. At first he explained he was not too concerned and that it was likely a hoax because the family was not in possession of cash anything close to $20,000. "But we're not going to take any chances. We need to protect our family and our home," explained Antonio. Frank and Roberto were assigned to continue guarding the front of the house from 10 p.m. to 5 a.m. while Antonio would watch the rear with Rex. Sleep would have to come from the time they came home from work to their armed watch time. No one was to shoot unless shot at. Vito would look out for Tony and they were not to go out of the house or yard without the company of an uncle.

"Pa why not ask Uncle Al for help," asked Roberto. "He would be happy to see who is responsible for this."

"No we take care of ourselves. We do not trouble him with matters we can handle ourselves," responded Antonio. "Franco has already asked to accompany Maria from work each night."

"How about the bike races Saturday night?" asked Vito. His mind was still on Gwen. He wanted desperately to have some romantic time with her.

The family's attention was immediately drawn to Vito in dead silence, and then all looked at Antonio. A surprised Antonio responded, "What, lives are at stake and you want to go to a bike race? No, no, no you will stay home when you are not in school."

The family meeting adjourned and most ate supper in the basement, the only real dining area big enough in the house. Supper was typical: spaghetti, Italian sausage, and Italian bread. Maria was escorted to Demark's by Franco. After supper Vito and Tony retired to their room in the attic. "Vito, I want to go to the bike races too and you aren't going without me, are you?" whispered Tony.

Vito was slipping on a night gown as he responded, "No, but you got to keep your mouth shut and stick with me and button your night drawers in the back. I'm tired of looking at your ass. I got a plan of getting out of here with Nanu's help."

Tony asked, "What plan?"

Vito had been thinking well before the family meeting. "Tony," Vito asked, "where besides this house is it safest for us?"

"In a jail, but Nanu would beat our asses," Tony said.

"No, no at church," answered Vito. "Holy Sacrament has a youth event this Saturday the same time as the bike race. We go to the event and slip out to the race, then return to church before Frank or Roberto come by to pick us up and then home we go."

With a big grin Tony replied, "Great idea Vito great idea."

"Good, did you brush your teeth? If not go down and brush them otherwise they'll look like crap and no girl will ever kiss you." Tony thought, I sure don't want teeth that look like crap. Vito then asked Tony to say his prayers on his way back from the bathroom.

On the second floor in the hallway were two large hollow statues on a chest of drawers: one of St Mary the Mother of Jesus and the second St. Joseph. It was a habit of the Cosenza brothers to say their evening prayers in front of the two saints. The statues had been permanent fixtures for over twenty years and a family superstition forbid they are moved.

Maria reported to work as usual, tied on her apron and was ready. The regular crowd gradually arrived, but there was a new customer, Tom O'Brien. He had been casing the Pontillo home and family activities. It only took him that first night to figure out where the mother of the two boys worked. With a polite tone Tom greeted Maria as she approached his table, "*Buonasera signorina.*"

Maria responded, *"Buonasera Signore* have you decided what you would like to drink and eat?"

"Ahh, just a cheap beer and a plate of fries."

"Si," responded Maria. "That's all we have now is cheap beer." She curiously looked at Tom again noticing his fair complexion and slight build and said, "You are not Italian."

"No I'm Irish," he answered. Soon she returned with an almost cold bottle of nonalcoholic beer and a glass. Tom took his con game seriously. He would at first establish a simple rapport with Maria and then get some information from her about her boys. By the third night Tom knew the boys' names, their ages, they liked bike races, the family attended Holy Sacrament Church and the boys would miss the bike races Saturday for a church event. He even knew what they looked like from pictures Maria had showed him.

Little did Tom know jealous eyes were watching. It was Bruno Salvatore, an old boyfriend of Maria's, but since she had married Angelo and had children, Bruno was just a casual friend. Bruno worked for the harbor master of the city harbor and on the side collected as a loan shark. Bruno felt a protective obligation to Maria since Angelo's death and was concerned about Tom. Tom had a thin face and reminded him of a rat. Bruno got up from his table and uninvited sat down at Tom's. Bruno stared at Tom; his dark eyes made the slightly built Tom very uncomfortable. Bruno placed his beer on the table and flexed his fingers and then seemingly looked at his exceptionally large hands. Bruno smiled and said, "When you have hands this big you call them paws."

Tom could feel his body sweat profusely, first his forehead and then his hands and arm pits. "So," Tom answered back, "you have very big hands, so what can I do for you?"

Bruno continued to stare making Tom very nervous and wishing he was elsewhere. Bruno laid a switch blade on the table and finally responded, "I see you talking too much to Maria. I think you are up to no good, and you remind me of a vermin that should be cut."

"Oh no *Signore* I'm just a customer that likes to drink cheap beer and listen to the fights in a nice neighborhood restaurant like this one." Tom looked at his watch and said, "Excuse me, I have to leave." He threw two dollars down, more than enough to pay for two beers, fries and a tip.

Maria walked over to Tom's table, picked up the empty beer bottle, a glass and the $2, wiped the table and turned to Bruno. "Did you meet the gentleman that was sitting here? He never did tell me his name."

"Yes," responded Bruno. "He seems like a polite man, but a little frail." Bruno then changed the subject and said, "You know I still care about you Maria."

Maria turned and momentarily stared at Bruno. "I know," she responded. Bruno was not only staring at Maria, he was also looking at her pin shaped like Cupid's bow. Bruno knew where the pin came from and that it was connected to him in a felonious way. The fact was Bruno seemed to have more cash on hand than the normal loan shark. Bruno got up from his chair and stepped outside just in time to see Tom get into a car with Illinois plates.

As Tom jumped into the passenger seat, he looked over his shoulder, and saw Bruno. "Holy shit," he blurted, panting heavily, "I'll never come to this place again."

"Calm down, calm down Tom," said a reassuring O'Brien.

"Okay Ned, give me a chance to collect my breath," Tom responded.

After a few moments O'Brien started scratching his head and then said, "So what did you learn?"

Tom wiped the sweat from his forehead and said, "I learned there is a big ass *Goombah* in there that wants to slice me up." Tom lit a cigarette and started puffing rapidly.

"No Tom. What did you learn about the kids!"

"Oh right, we got one chance this week to grab one or both of the boys but it will be tough. It will have to be in or near Holy Sacrament Church during a youth event. They like bike races and they're Saturday too. We'll have to get very lucky. Right now I think we check out the church. I got an angle. Maria gave me some detail about the youth event, so one or two of us pose as new parishioners interested in youth activities. We attend the event and seize the chance to lure one of them outside and then we grab him."

"Sounds easy enough," responded O'Brien. "What then?"

Tom had it all worked out. "Then we take the kid south to my place, we hole up with the kid, and this time I call Pontillo, then it's his turn to make a move and I'll do the talking."

The next few nights were uneventful for the Pontillos. However, Antonio was still concerned that the danger wasn't over. Every moment he wondered how he would respond to new demands and from time to time he would check on his two grandsons. Vito reassured Antonio, "Nanu we'll be fine. Tony and I haven't left the yard, so we look forward to going to church tomorrow."

"*Si, si,*" responded Antonio who wasn't any less concerned, church was the only place he would allow them to go. He couldn't understand why others in the family didn't seem as concerned. Perhaps it was because they had never personally experienced the evil of two bit gangsters, or worse, the Mob or the likes of the Black Hand. When he was ten, he worked for a fifth of a lira a day in his uncle's market place in Naples. There he stocked shelves with produce, swept the floor, cleaned vegetables and helped customers. From time to time rough looking characters would talk to his uncle. When Antonio asked his uncle who they were he simply said they were collecting insurance. The Black Hand was demanding a large percentage of his uncle's profits, and they told him he needed to be a good patron and contribute. Hard times came across the country and his uncle couldn't make a full payment. It got worse for his uncle; he had his vegetables as low priced as he could. When he fell behind further after three visits the thugs returned. Antonio's uncle commanded him to go to the back. Antonio stood terrified behind several empty wooden boxes as the thugs first roughed his uncle up. When his uncle fought back a thug drew a stiletto and stabbed his uncle again and again. One of the thugs said, "*Pol morire una mille morte.*" Antonio was helpless as he tried to stop the bleeding. He watched his uncle bleed to death. The authorities did nothing because they too were part of the corruption. An older Antonio was wise; he knew enough to show respect, but not to ever show fear or let on that he knew too much. The last position he would ever want to be in was to owe a favor to a Mob boss. It wasn't that he did not like Alvano, he just didn't like his business because he took advantage of man's weaknesses.

CHAPTER 5

Tony's Abduction

"So this is Holy Sacrament," Rizzo said. Rizzo and Tom looked up at the tall steeple and the beautiful mosaic widows. The two men walked to the parish office and introduced themselves using fictitious names. There they met Father Falbo who introduced the two to his staff. The men told the priest and the staff secretary they were new in town, from Pennsylvania, and wanted to join an active youth-oriented parish.

Father Falbo was always eager to show off God's house and was excited the two had families and were interested in youth activities. "Why you're in luck my sons, we have a special annual youth event tomorrow afternoon--here is a program." Father Falbo couldn't help himself and explained the days' program. Father Falbo went on and on and ended with a description of the Church Bazaar being organized for the following week.

In his raspy voice Rizzo quickly asked, "Tell me Father will there be games of chance at the Bazaar?"

Father Falbo smiled. "Why yes, legitimate games of chance. We even have a review board to ensure that they are all honest."

"Great," Tom responded. "We need to leave, we'll see you tomorrow."

"Wonderful," said Father Falbo as he shook their hands.

Tom wiped his forehead as if he were stressed, chuckled and said, "Wow! I'd almost rather deal with the *Goombah* in Demark's and get the crap beat out of me than listen to anymore church bullshit."

Rizzo was surprised and said, "Watch it Tom, you don't want to piss God off or we'll really be in deep shit."

"Okay so let's head back to State Line," ordered Tom. The two reached Tom's rental where O'Brien was waiting. They were prepared: ample provisions for a couple nights, Pontillo's phone number, a big rug, and rope to subdue one of the Cosenza boys and a plan that they believed would work.

For the Cosenza brothers Saturday did not come soon enough. Vito would get a chance to experience real romance with Gwen without an escort or interruption and Tony was excited to see the cyclers' crash and fight. He didn't care who won. Vito was just finishing with his monthly shave when he looked at Tony and said, "Wash your face and hands and put on a clean shirt that has all the buttons."

Tony followed his brother's instructions when Frank shouted, "*Fretta, fretta.*"

"Here we come," shouted Tony. Frank and the boys loaded into the family car and Roberto drove them to Holy Sacrament Church. Tom and Rizzo were also arriving at the church.

"Okay we'll see you at eight here in front of the church, no later," said Roberto.

"Maybe I should stay around?" whispered Frank to Roberto. Vito's heart sank. Once one of his uncles made up their minds they were done thinking.

Vito didn't want to panic and carefully responded, "Yes, I understand, but Father Falbo will be here."

The Pontillo brothers looked at each other and Frank said, "Okay." The two boys entered the church gym. Vito walked directly to the basketballs and began shooting. Within seconds an older lady told him there would be time for basketball later.

Dozens of pre-teen and teen age boys and girls were in the gym. The noise of high pitched young voices was deafening. "That's them," whispered Tom, "the two with the blue shirts."

The first thing that came to Rizzo's mind was how big Tony was. "Holy shit," he whispered to Tom. "The young one is bigger than the two of us." Rizzo and Tom stayed close to the two brothers, but not too close to catch their attention.

A few moments passed until Father Falbo saw Tom and Rizzo. He approached them and asked, "Are your children here?"

Rizzo was caught off guard and started to stutter when Tom said, "No they're sick."

"That's a shame, because the kids really enjoy these events," replied Father Falbo.

Nearby, Vito looked slyly at Tony and said, "Follow me." They walked down a long hallway to a door that led them to the back of the church. The boys slipped out and ran west as fast as they could to the cycle rink a few blocks away. Their path led them to 31st Street, past a large wooded area with a stream at the bottom, and then a large bowl-like valley. It was perfect for a large cycle track where the fans could watch from above on a grassy hillside. Hundreds of bike fans were already watching the races. But Vito and Gwen had a plan where to meet. Tom and Rizzo saw the boys leave and immediately jumped in their car with O'Brien and pursued the Cosenza brothers. The goons saw the boys just as they reached the track entrance.

"This will be perfect," reported Rizzo. "There is a wooded access road above the track and event area. We'll drive through it." Rizzo followed with, "The road is concealed all the way by trees and the road leads to a series of shit houses. We park the sedan in the woods, get one of the boys near the car, and we grab him." The trio drove the sedan down the access road slapping tree branches all the way. The second race had started when Tom and Rizzo began searching for either of the boys when Tony was spotted alone. Vito had left him momentarily to find Gwen, promising he would be right back.

Rizzo approached Tony, who was really into the race. Rizzo spoke up in a raspy voice, "Tony Cosenza, your brother Vito needs you for a minute, nothing serious."

"Who are you?" responded Tony.

Rizzo replied, "A friend of your uncle's, you look like your dad."

"Where's Vito?"

With a convincing voice Rizzo said, "He's over by the privies, over there. In a few minutes you can come back here with him." Rizzo and Tony walked to the privies. Tony became nervous, it just didn't seem right; there was no one else, but another man. "Now where did that boy go," asked Rizzo. "There he is around back." No sooner had the two walked to the back when the other two thugs came quickly. O'Brien grabbed Tony from behind while Tom stuffed a rag in Tony's mouth. Rizzo grabbed his two feet and they struggled carrying him to the car. Tony slammed O'Brien with an elbow twice and kicked Rizzo in the crotch. Tom looped a rope around him several times, bound his hands and feet then struck him several times in the stomach, knocking the wind out of him. They wrapped him in a blanket and flopped Tony into the trunk and slammed it shut. "Did anyone see us?" asked Rizzo.

"No I don't think so," responded Tom as he searched the grounds, looking for anyone that may have witnessed the abduction. Tom followed up with more instructions. "Drive straight out onto 31st Street then Green Bay Road and south to State Line. We'll let the Pontillos think about this for a short time." Within thirty minutes they were at Tom's and had Tony tied up in the basement. The three stared at Tony, who didn't whimper.

"Kid I ought to give you a lick for this shiner of mine," said O'Brien. "We may be two bit hoods, but we're not kid killers, let's hope all goes well."

Several teardrops came from Tony's eyes as the reality of what had happened struck him. He mumbled through the rag in his mouth saying his nanu was not a rich man and that they'd wish they were dead when his nanu and uncles catch them.

Vito returned with Gwen ten minutes later, to where he had left Tony. The crowd was screaming as the bikers came around the closest curve. "Where can he be?" questioned Vito. Vito's first thought was another road block to a few moments of passion with Gwen.

"Let's split up and look for him," said Gwen.

"Yeah let's look maybe--he's with friends," responded Vito.

A stranger yelled above the crowd noise, "Say are you looking for that big kid that was sitting there? He walked up to the shit houses with some guy that said he knows his uncles. He had a funny voice like a sick guy."

"Thanks," shouted Vito. "Let's look for him on top of the bowl."

Gwen reached for Vito's hand, held it tight and tried to be reassuring. "Sure Vito, don't worry, he'll be around."

As they hustled uphill, Vito filled her in on the threatening letter, what had happened at their house and school. They reached the privies and Tony was not to be found.

They spent the next hour looking for him. They searched together, asked friends of Tony's, and explored the woods only to find the high grass had been recently driven over. The compacted grass was a defining clue—someone may have abducted Tony. "Holy Mother of God, they got my brother and it's my fault, it's my entire fault," explained Vito. The two had to split up, Gwen joined her friends and promised not to mention the abduction and Vito returned to Holy Sacrament Church.

Vito walked into the Holy Sacrament gym just as the youth event ended. He was in tears and was noticed by Father Falbo. As the crowd cleared the church Father Falbo walked to Vito and with a sensitive smile he asked what was troubling him. Vito unloaded, starting with his deception of his family to see his girlfriend and ending with the abduction of Tony. "It's my fault Father I'm a worthless piece of crap and I deserve punishment. I love my little brother and now I let him down, I should have stuck with him -- no, we should have stayed here at church." Father Falbo tried to console him.

A few moments had passed when Frank stepped into the gym. Father Falbo looked at Frank with his arms around Vito. "Frank we have disturbing news. Tony was abducted by men of the devil."

"What, while at church here in the gym, in front of all of you?" Frank yelled.

"No my son, it's a detailed story some of which you already know. Please let me return with you to your home first," said Father Falbo. Father Falbo followed the Pontillos home in his new Cadillac.

Questions kept focusing on Vito on the way home. Why this and why not that and why did you? Vito thought his heart had stopped, yet his aching gut assured him he was not spared the mercy of dying right there. Antonio was listening to the radio when Roberto shouted, "Pa turn the radio off, we have disturbing news."

The radio was turned off and the two women at home stood up seeing faces of despair: the brothers, Vito, Father Falbo, but no Tony.

"Where's Tony?" screamed Giovanna.

"Please, please everyone sit down, despite the sad news we must stay calm. I must help Vito explain what has happened," said Father Falbo. "He is very disturbed."

"Where is Tony? What has happened?" growled Antonio.

"Please, please again let me help explain," said Father Falbo. Just then there was a knock at the door.

"Who could that be?" whispered Giovanna.

"Roberto, *la porta, la porta*," directed Antonio.

Roberto opened the door and, it was Franco. "I was watering my garden when I saw you returning with Father Falbo and without Tony. I also heard screaming. Can I help?"

"Please sit down Franco," asked Father Falbo. Father Falbo went on to explain what Vito had told him in the best detail he could and ended with, we must go to the authorities for help. Vito tried talking, but could not say more than two words before breaking down.

"Roberto please get Maria, she must know this news," requested Antonio. Roberto dashed out the door to Demark's to get Maria.

Just as the two arrived home from Demark's, Frank began to feel guilty for not staying with the boys. Maria was in tears when Frank said, "It was my fault, we were going to stay at the youth event, but decided the boys would be fine. Vito is not to blame and neither is Tony, they are children and we're the adults."

"No, no it's my fault for letting them go," added Antonio then asking. "What did they look like, did anyone see them?"

"Yes," said Vito, "but all I know is one of the guys had a funny voice." Maria was so distraught she couldn't talk for twenty minutes.

"How would the thugs know they were going to church or the bike races?" asked Franco. "I did not know this and I am your neighbor." They all looked at each other wondering, yes how would they know?

Maria sat huddled with her mother and sister and responded, "My dear Jesus, I am to blame. I talk too much. There was a new customer last week. I showed him pictures of the boys. I told him about the church event and where they would be, I told, I told him, it's my fault for being so *stupido*."

A few more minutes passed with everyone contemplating what should have happened when Father Falbo said, "This is all strange. Two men approached me during the week and were interested in joining our congregation and were especially interested in the youth events. They were there this afternoon, but had no children. I asked where their kids were and one was surprised and the second said they were sick."

Maria immediately said, "Father what did they look like?" Father Falbo described them and Maria explained the man with the normal voice fit the description of the new customer.

Underneath Antonio's calm he was furious that someone had now threatened the life of a family member. Several hours went by before Father Falbo once more requested a call to the authorities. Antonio reached for the phone just as Franco said, "Wait Antonio. Out of respect, Father, they will not be of help."

Antonio put the phone down and said, "*Si*, you're right. They would do nothing. I will go to Al. He will know what to do, *silenzio*, no one say a word of this."

"*Si*," said Franco. "Let me escort you. For something like this it's not too late." Franco added, "Besides it's Saturday evening, he will not be at home, but I know where he will be."

It took a few minutes for Tony's eyes to adjust to the darkness and try to make sense out of what had happened. It was cold, dark and dingy in the basement he was tied up in. The only light was from under the cellar door. The basement had no windows, but he could smell coal. So there had to be a coal chute to deliver coal through for the furnace. Tony thought how much he missed his family and his pa -- why did he have to die? Before long the door opened and one of his abductors stepped down into the basement, pulled a light chain and stared at Tony. The chunky O'Brien threw his spent cigarette in Tony's direction, chuckled and said, "Look you little smart ass, you see my eye, no one has ever made it look like this. I ought to belt you for it, but I won't. If your family follows orders you'll be out safe in a couple days. If not, no telling what we do. You may just rot down here." O'Brien laughed again and walked back up the stairs leaving the light on. Tony looked around and there was the coal chute at the top of a pile of coal. There was plenty of trash around and maybe something to cut the rope binding his feet and hands. He was tied to one the beams supporting the floor. Through the creaking floor he could hear the goons above pacing, playing cards, drinking and trying to decide what to do next. He could barely make out the words "phone call" and "tomorrow." Tony spun around the pole and saw a bag behind him. Tony scooted back around just in time to look up and see Tom turn off the basement stairs light.

CHAPTER 6

Alvano and the Problem

Franco drove as fast as he could, taking the shortest route to a speakeasy on the south side of Chicago. To Antonio it seemed to take an eternity. Franco parked the car and said, "Antonio wait here, I'll return for you soon." From the outside it looked like any other hardware store. Franco walked to a side door located in a narrow alley between two buildings. Fifteen minutes went by before Franco returned with Mean Mike. Mean Mike greeted Antonio and assisted the older man out of the car and escorted him to the side of the building. A small peep door opened at the side door. The trio walked in and then to a table near a stage where Al Alvano and several of his business associates sat. The joint was a cloud of smoke and a band was playing jazz music. "Al, may we have a moment with you," requested Franco.

Alvano looked up, smiled, and although he had a good idea of what happened, he just spoke with Franco. Alvano asked Antonio and Franco to make themselves comfortable. "Antonio," Alvano said, "I will introduce you to my business associates. This is Sam Del Vechio, Jim Ronzonelli, and the pale guy is Alex Kaiser. My friends, you all know my brother but this is a dear friend Antonio Pontillo." Alvano took out a fresh cigar and bit the end off. A Wise Guy was there immediately to lite it. Alvano smiled and said, "*Gracia*." He then turned back to Antonio and offered him a cigar, which was accepted. Then Alvano said with a firm voice, "You can be assured these men are well trusted. You are wise to come to me. I know you are a proud man. Understand I take the abduction of Tony personal and I will not sleep until he is safe with you and the scum that took him understand what a mistake they made. Did you bring the letter they sent you?"

"*Si* it's in my pocket," said Antonio. Antonio drew the letter from his pocket handed it to Alvano and he handed it to Kaiser. Antonio made a fist with both hands and showing his anger saying, "There should be no compromise with their life. They chose to take one of ours and we need *morta* for justice." Neither Alvano nor Franco was surprised to see the anger in Antonio's heart. They knew Antonio was a gentle man, yet in his youth very formidable and backed down from no-one.

Kaiser looked at the letter near a candle and said, "It's post marked Waukegan." Then he looked at the hand writing and the paper and started to laugh. "Fools," he said. "It's written on very cheap paper, the kind they give to inmates in Joliet or Cook County, the letter is poorly written and look at the envelope." Kaiser placed the letter and envelope back on the table.

A smile came to Alvano's face as he puffed his Cuban cigar and said, "Already we have made progress Antonio; we will have Tony to you and your family and soon. Get Antonio a drink, a cocktail or *vino?*"

"*Vino per piacere,*" said Antonio.

"What else do you know Antonio?" asked Kaiser. Antonio gave him as much information as he could remember. An important clue was the goon with a raspy voice. "I want to know why they think you have 50 Gs," asked Kaiser.

"It is a mystery to me other than we have five in the family with jobs," explained Antonio. "Many families are suffering because they have no work."

"May I speak?" asked Mean Mike.

"*Si,*" said Alvano.

"Antonio, did you know about an old rumor that Angelo robbed a big jewelry store back east, fenced the loot and gave you thousands of bucks before he died?"

Antonio sat upright in his chair and said, "No, no I know of nothing like that. We did not know what Angelo did for a living and never asked.

He helped us with cash from time to time and provided for his family. He never gave me money like that!"

Mean Mike added, "I thought so. I think some chump started the rumor and those goons heard the same rumor."

"Franco, when Antonio is finished please take him home," Alvano said. "Mike, you find Salerno and follow them home." Antonio finished his *vino* and kissed the back of Alvano's hand and thanked him for the help. With a reassuring confidence Alvano told Antonio not to worry, to expect a phone call from the goons, to stall for time and then to let him know through Franco any new information.

Antonio's eyes were glazed with shame and anger. His shame: for allowing the thugs the opportunity to abduct the youngest member of the family, and anger for vengeance toward those who took Tony.

Antonio turned and looked back at Alvano. "When you find the demons that took our Tony you send them to hell, or if you choose not to, I will, even at the thought of burning in hell."

All became very quiet upstairs in the old farmhouse. O'Brien and Rizzo were snoozing in the living room and Tom was in his upstairs bedroom. For Tony it was time to make his move. He scooted back and slid his torso down the post as far as he could. With his long legs he could feel the bag in the dark and there was something hard in it. He used his legs like tongs and pulled the bag closer and closer to his crotch and then he lifted one leg and kicked it to his side. It was tiresome so he rested a few moments. When he heard footsteps above, moving toward the basement door, he scooted back around just in time. The basement door opened, and this time it was Rizzo. Rizzo pulled the light chain and looked at Tony still bound and gagged. Rizzo was emotionless, pulled the light chain again, turned and walked back up the stairs. If it were not for Tony's size Rizzo might have seen the bag behind him.

Tony was sweating like he had never sweat before; he was fighting for his life. He had heard abduction stories and seldom did a paid ransom make a difference in a life being spared. Tony was barely able to feel the bag with his fingers, but managed to seize the edge of the bag and then tear it with his thumbs and fingers. There was a booze bottle in it. He took the bottle by the head and broke it on the bag to muffle the sound, and then cut at the rope on his wrists. He cut the top side of his wrists several times, it didn't matter. After thirty minutes he cut through the rope. It would be daylight soon so he had to hurry. He pulled the gag from his mouth took a deep breath, untied his feet and his body rope. He walked cautiously in the dark as to not trip onto the coal pile.

He slowly crawled up the coal pile to avoid making any noise, slipping frequently. He finally managed to reach the coal chute door. He lifted the lever holding it shut and started to squeeze through the door. The sun was rising and he could see a corn field on the other side of a grove of trees he could run to. He just had to get his hips through the opening so he kicked hard with his feet trying to get some momentum to thrust himself through. There was a pop that sounded like a gunshot. It wasn't: his foot had hit a light bulb.

"What the hell was that?" shouted Rizzo. "Hell it's the kid." Rizzo jumped off the couch he was dozing on and as he ran to the basement door he shouted, "Go outside." Tony had just managed to work his way through the opening with that last kick. He jumped to his feet and ran as fast as he could for the corn field and thought, I'm gonna make it I'm faster than they are. But the early morning dew on the grass made it slippery. It was like one of those nightmares where you run as fast as you can but don't gain any ground. As he reached the edge of the farmhouse lawn he felt something hard strike his right calf throwing him off and to the ground. Rizzo grabbed him and then O'Brien helped hold him down. Now Tony could feel the wet dew on his body as it soaked through his clothes.

"Next time we keep this punk in sight, day and night," yelled Tom.

"Screw you, you morons," shouted Tony just as he kicked Tom in the thigh. Tom was delighted in his chance to deck Tony with a punch to his left cheek and then one to his side.

Tony fell limp when O'Brien yelled, "Lay off, that's enough he's just a punk kid." Tom held back on his third swing.

When Tony regained his breath Tom greeted him. "Well, we asked fifty thousand dollars for your sorry ass. Now we'll see if your family gives a shit about you."

"My family doesn't even have fifty dollars," responded Tony.

"I like to play cards smart guy, do you?" replied Tom. Before Tony could answer Tom added, "I like to play poker and I think you're bluffing and your family will come up with it one way or another. Your dad left your granddad with thousands of bucks."

"My pa didn't leave us with a dime, what are you talking about?" barked a confused Tony.

Rizzo walked closer to Tony and said, "Your pa was a big time crook, didn't you know that?"

Tony shifted his body to get a little more comfortable and said, "You're full of crap." Then Tony thought he would turn the table and said, "Say aren't you chumps afraid?"

"What?" responded O'Brien. "Of who? You?"

Tony assertively answered, "No, no, not me smart guy. I don't think you understand who you are messing with. I think you should be scared. You would be if you knew what I know."

"So just what is that smart ass?" asked O'Brien as he started to scratch his head.

Tom spun to his left and said, "Ned quit talking to the little piece of shit."

Rizzo interrupted, "No, I want to hear what he has to say. So go on, tell us more, you have my attention."

Tony just smiled and said nothing. He knew he had them concerned and would have them scared and arguing in a minute. After a few more moments of silence Tony said, "Well you need to understand my family is in good with Al Alvano, you know the Mobster. When Uncle Al finds out what you goons have done he'll come after you and you'll all get whacked. Besides Alvano is my brother's Godfather, that's a big deal to Italians and he will be furious. But if you let me go I think he would back off."

"If we let you go would you put in a good word for us?" Rizzo said.

"Sure," replied Tony.

Tom glared at Rizzo, then turned and looked at Tony and said, "Kid you're as full of bullshit as Rizzo." Tom turned back to look at Rizzo and said, "Rizzo for the last time shut up."

Rizzo nervously lit a cigarette and started pacing. He was worried and he turned toward Tom and O'Brien and said, "You know guys maybe we should call this whole thing off. Alvano is not the forgiving type and I know this from experience. He'll stop at nothing to kill us. He has connections all over the Midwest and the East. He'd find us."

"Yeah you got something Rizzo. I was afraid we'd mess with the wrong *Goombah*!" answered O'Brien.

Tom also started pacing back and forth when he shouted, "You two are chicken shits. You know that! Ned, I'm surprised you don't have the backbone. You chumps wanted me to help. Now you want to back out because you're scared of this bullshit story from a punk kid!"

"Kiss my ass Tom," yelled O'Brien. An argument followed and went on for ten minutes before Tom pulled his .38 and threatened to shoot anyone that backed out.

"Are you out of your mind Tom? We are messing with the wrong guy! Maybe I'm not so smart, but this I do know, Alvano has whacked at least a dozen guys like us, you hear me?" shouted Rizzo.

Rizzo may have convinced O'Brien, but Tom waived his pistol and said, "You see this .38? It's my vote and there is no turning back! We got the kid and we get the money!"

Tom pulled the hammer back and aimed the .38 at Rizzo. O'Brien raised his hands in the air as to give up and pleaded, "Tom put the gun down. Please put it down. We'll finish the job like we planned."

O'Brien and Rizzo shoved Tony into the downstairs bed room and tied Tony's arms and legs spread eagle to bed posts. As Rizzo was folding a towel to gag Tony, Tony whispered, "I know how you'll die."

"You really are a smart ass!" said Rizzo. But Rizzo was still nervous and he knew the final outcome would be the end of his life.

Alvano was at his office desk staring at a picture of the Last Supper on a wall to the right of his desk. He wondered about the treason in Judas's heart and if he was eventually forgiven by Christ. His daydreaming was interrupted by a knock at the door—it was Kaiser. "Let him in Mike."

"*Buongiorno* Don Alvano," greeted Kaiser.

"*Si Buongiorno*. We need to move as quickly as possible. These goons are amateurs and I'm concerned that they may panic and do something even more stupid," responded Alvano.

"Yes I agree; we need your most competent men on this, I have a plan," answered Kaiser.

Alvano came back, "*Si* that is why you will lead the search."

"I expected I would. First we check the parole records over the last four months: who has been released and who is in parole violation. Then we check records at Waupon, Joliet, Cook County, and Indiana, we send out your most competent men and talk to our most reliable informants -- it's important they do not draw any attention to our search. We keep in touch with Pontillo and your brother and pay attention to the smallest detail. They will call Pontillo soon. We instruct him to stall the first time and follow a script I have prepared for him. He must be careful and use these words," explained Kaiser.

"*Buono*," answered Alvano. "Enrico, I want you Mike, Salerno and Castellanos to listen very carefully to *Signor* Kaiser."

Enrico "The Assassin" Parillo grabbed the lapels on his suit and nodded his head in approval and said, "*Si*."

Alvano said, "Tony is my Godson's brother and I will bring these worthless pieces of shit to our justice, remember that Enrico." While Mean Mike had a reputation as a hard guy, Enrico The Assassin Parillo was intelligent and exceptionally cruel in his dealings for the Family. Enrico delighted in another opportunity to punish or whack someone.

The Pontillos sat in their living room waiting for the phone call. The women had wept so much through the night they were exhausted. Vito finally fell asleep on the floor while his uncles rested in chairs. Franco was there with his wife. The dead silence was broken by a knock at the door. Everyone jumped with nervous anticipation and looked to the door. Someone shouted *la porta*. Roberto opened it, and it was Father Falbo. He stepped in, greeted everyone and gave the family a blessing, Communion, led them in prayer for Tony's safe return and then left for the 8:30 Mass.

Just as Father Falbo walked out the door the phone rang. Antonio lifted the speaker and ear piece and said, "*Si*."

"Who's talking?" asked the caller.

"It's me Antonio Pontillo."

"So you went to the cops!"

"No I did not," answered Antonio.

"Good," said Tom. "We got the kid and he's okay for now, but he is a pain in the ass. You got twenty-four hours to come up with $50,000 in small unmarked bills."

Antonio followed his script roughly saying, "I do not have that kind of money and it's a Sunday."

Tom abruptly ended the conversation. "That's your problem," and hung up.

Antonio looked at his family. "They want $50,000 now and in twenty-four hours."

Franco immediately said, "No, no Antonio, Al will get you the 50 grand. I'll let him know what the ransom is, all will be fine. They'll talk about you having to have more time and they'll give you more time, I'm sure."

The phone rang again and it was Tom. He told Antonio he now had till Tuesday night and no more stalling.

Within hours Alvano's men had the name of every man released from four state prisons in the tri-state area: recently released, those still on probation and those in parole violation. With these lists in hand they sought out reliable informants. Most were of little value. Franco reported to Alvano and Kaiser what the thugs said with the first and second phone calls.

Carmine The Weasel Francisco stared at a large crack in the ceiling of his bunk room. It had been six days since Carmine was released from the Cook County Jail. He was staying at a south side flop house for a dollar a night waiting for a break and wondering who would come after him first. His living since his release from Cook County was bumming nickels and dimes by day on a street corner across from the Carlton. His biggest hit was $65 in a purse he stole the night before. He thought there was no way he could ever set it straight with the Mob; he had violated their trust. The best thing he could do was leave town and soon. He was so frustrated with life he would welcome death.

A loud knock interrupted Carmine's daydreaming. "Weasel let me in, it's Mike Pontillo."

"What the hell do you want?" shouted Carmine.

"Do I bust the door down or do you let me in?" answered Mean Mike. Carmine looked at the window and opened it. Damn he thought, I jump from here and I'm smashed like a bug or open the door and get all busted up and maybe killed.

He turned to the door and yelled, "Are you going to kill me?"

In a calm voice Mean Mike explained, "No, you know better. I've never killed anyone in broad daylight."

Carmine opened the door and saw Enrico The Assassin Parillo standing behind Mean Mike. He turned and ran to the open window and just as he was ready to leap slipped on a rug. He looked up and cried out loud, "You're here to kill me!"

Enrico picked him up by the shirt and said, "It depends on you. Don Alvano needs some information and we thought you could help."

Carmine felt a little cocky and responded, "What is it worth?"

Mean Mike looked at Enrico and frowned. Enrico pulled out his stiletto and popped it open. He pulled Carmine's sleeve up and cut a few hairs off his arm and whispered, "Wrong answer."

Carmine fainted only to have a glass of water poured on his face. "Just kidding," Carmine chirped. "How can I help?" Before the Wise Guys finished explaining what had happened and that one goon had a raspy voice Carmine interrupted them. "I know who you want." He went further to describe what went down weeks earlier in Cook County. "That's Sam Rizzo with the raspy voice and his buddy Ned O'Brien. O'Brien has a brother he may be staying with." Carmine had no idea where the brother lived or his first name. Carmine felt lucky to satisfy the two Wise Guys and thought he would see if they could help him. "Boys," he said. "I asked nothing for myself and gave you good information. Suppose you could ask the Don to cut me some slack and just find me a legit job?"

"Sure," said Enrico as he handed him a C note. "We'll see what we can do, meanwhile you keep your mouth shut or you'll sleep with the fishes."

Carmine gulped. He was absolutely terrified and said, "I'm not going anywhere till I hear back from you."

"*Buono*," replied Mean Mike.

All of Alvano's Wise Guys reported to Kaiser with what they had learned. Mean Mike and Enrico had the best information while Nick Pellegrino still had an assignment to complete. The mystery as to who the abductors might be was falling into place quicker than expected. Kaiser examined all the clues and said, "Now Nick first thing tomorrow pay one of our friends at the Department of Transportation a visit and find out what kind of a car this O'Brien may have, where he lives, and the license plate." Monday morning Nick returned with a list. There were dozens of O'Briens who had registered cars in the several counties in Chicagoland and unless they could get a first name they were stuck.

Kaiser called Antonio and explained that great progress had been made. They needed more time. One of the goons was a Sam Rizzo and a second was a Ned O'Brien and he was likely staying with a brother. The problem was they didn't know the first name of O'Brien's brother or where he lived and couldn't be sure that was where Tony was being held. Antonio would have to stall again for one more day and explain he was trying to locate a brother in New York who would have the money wired to him. On cue Tom called again to make pick-up arrangements. He bought Antonio's story and the deadline was reluctantly extended another twenty-four hours.

"I just gave the old man another twenty-four hours. I told you the punk was bullshitting us," said a heated Tom. "If Pontillo was such buddies with Alvano he'd have the money. Instead he says he needs time to get the 50 Gs from a brother in New York."

"I think you're right," said O'Brien.

"Don't be too sure," commented Rizzo.

"Rizzo, make yourself useful and brew some coffee and then check on the punk again," commanded Tom.

Maria returned to work and was very distraught. Demark noticed her tenseness and after Maria explained what had happened he told her she could go home. Maria declined for several reasons; sitting home would not help and she needed to work to make a living.

Not long after Maria started her evening shift Bruno stopped in earlier than usual for his usual beer and dinner. "Maria you look very sad. Could I be of any help?" asked Bruno.

Maria explained, "No I don't think you can. Remember the guy that you said looked frail?"

"Sure," answered Bruno, "I followed the little creep out the door."

"What did you see?" replied Maria. "We think he and another thug grabbed our Tony and they're asking a ransom."

Bruno got up off his stool and became animated. He pointed to the door and said, "I'm so sorry to hear that. I knew he was up to no good! I followed him out the door because I was curious. I saw him get into a piece of crap 22 Chevy coupe with Illinois plates. I even remember part of the license number, it was CH332 something." Maria was excited. She kissed Bruno and ran out the door and home to report the number.

"Where the hell is she off to?" said a surprised Demark.

"I think home," said Bruno. "I think I just said something very important. Tony was abducted by some goons and one of them may have been that creepy Tom that was in here a few days ago."

Antonio immediately called Franco and he called Kaiser to deliver the new information. Nick quickly called their informant with the Illinois Department of Transportation, with a description of the car and a partial plate number. Within a short time the informant provided the needed information, despite it being a Sunday. The Alvano gang had the name of the owner of the car and the address of a Tom O'Brien.

"He has a rural box number 7663 on State Line Road and is driving a 22 Chevy coupe, very good," said Kaiser. "Now we have your boys case the place out. Enrico this will be your job."

"*Si,*" answered Enrico. "I thought about casing the place too, but after we are sure he is on State Line. Here is an idea, before we case the place we have a couple whores drive to the place and get a layout of the inside. They can use the line they're lost. They check it out and then tell us what they seen"

"Not a bad idea. Do we have anyone with the guts?" offered Kaiser.

"Sure we do: Gail, the colored girl, and Lois. They handle our roughest customers," responded Enrico. "They got a set of, well you know, they're tough as nails."

Gwen could not help herself. She crossed the street to the Italian side and knocked at the Pontillos' side door.

"I'll get it," shouted Rose. Rose opened the door. "Gwen what are you doing on this side of the street?"

"Oh please, I need to see Vito, please, I won't be long," responded Gwen.

Rose called for Vito. He was surprised. He walked down the stairs to the side door. "Hi Gwen, you sure look nice!" Vito's heart began to pound as he slowly took Gwen into his arms. She smelled of heaven and her soft skin made him feel good, but the abduction of Tony spoiled the moment.

"I haven't said a word to anyone and I was worried about you. I know how much you love Tony," Gwen said.

"I'm fine. We have friends trying to find him and the goons that grabbed him," answered Vito.

Tears came from Gwen's eyes. "I hope they find Tony. I have to go." She started to turn and then quickly kissed Vito on the cheek and returned home.

Gail and Lois were up to the task of deception. To them it was suspense and intrigue. They had no clue why they were to get the inside layout of a little old farmhouse. Enrico thought they would be safer not knowing. But knowing they would be dealing with dangerous and possibly armed thugs made it all the more suspenseful.

Mean Mike and Enrico drove slowly down State Line Road and easily found Box 7663. There it was: a dumpy little two story farmhouse in need of paint and repairs. There was an equally old barn also in poor condition. After finding the farmhouse they sent the gals in. Gail and Lois had driven separately in a snazzy little Nash. They drove by once and then drove up the long driveway, then parked and paused to not create a situation of surprise for the inhabitants of the house. Together they walked to the front door and Gail knocked.

An ongoing card game was interrupted by the knock. "Who the hell's that at the door?" whispered Tom. He then walked to the room Tony was in and closed the door.

O'Brien peaked out the front window shades and saw the Nash first. He could barely see the two women because the sun was in his eyes. When he could see them he whispered, "Oh my, it's two broads. Are they ever stacked."

"I'll go back with the kid," said Tom. "Rizzo, answer the door."

Because the curtains were drawn the women could not see into the house until Rizzo opened the door. "Hi sweetheart we're lost and need some help finding some friends," said Lois as she pushed her way in. "Can we step out of the sun?"

"Sure, but you gotta leave soon. So who are you looking for?" asked Rizzo. O'Brien stood by with his mouth open and trying to avoid a direct stare at the women's partially exposed breasts.

Lois asked in a sultry voice, "We're looking for a couple of Johns on State Line but maybe you boys want some company. We could make you feel real good--what do you think honey?"

While Lois had Rizzo and O'Brien's attention Gail made a quick inventory of the lower floor. She could see a stove, ice box, four chairs, a table with a complement of flies, a disgusting couch and three doors, two closed, one open door leading into a bathroom, and a stairway to the upstairs. She also saw on the table what appeared to be a revolver partially hidden by a newspaper, a card game and three cups of coffee.

Rizzo was tempted but knew better and said, "I'm new here and don't know any neighbors so I can't help, but good luck," as he moved them back out the door. Then he whispered, "Come back in a couple days."

Rizzo watched as Lois and Gail walked to the Nash and drove back to State Line, driving slowly to avoid giving the appearance of fleeing. The woman rendezvoused with Enrico and Mean Mike and they all returned to Kaiser with the lowdown of the house. They weren't sure if Tony was up or downstairs. Most important was there was no uncertainty; the goons had at least one gun.

The phone rang at the Pontillos' at precisely 5:00 p.m. and Antonio answered. "Hello this is Antonio."

"Hello Antonio, do you have the 50 grand in small bills?" asked Tom.

"*Si*, I have the money, but if you harm my grandson your suffering by my hands will be worse than that in hell."

"Fine," responded Tom, "Tony, is okay, but don't threaten me again. Now listen and listen good. I don't want any screw ups. There is a Milwaukee run of the Northshore train at 9:00 tonight at the Kenosha station. You be there at 8:45."

"*Si*," responded a heated Antonio.

"We're not done yet. Bring it in a small suitcase. You wait for the train at the north end of the dock. When the train approaches at 200 feet, set the suitcase down and step to the left side of it."

"That's all?" asked Antonio.

"That's all, but if you screw up the kid is a goner and I ain't fooling--we can't wait to get rid of him one way or another," said Tom.

After hanging up Antonio looked to Franco who had stayed with him through the day and explained what Tom had said. "I don't understand? Maybe he'll be on the train," said Franco. "I have the money we just need to find a small suitcase."

In a soft tone Antonio added, "I have a small suitcase."

"Now I need to call Al," said Franco.

Within an hour of the visit to the farmhouse the Wise Guys and women reported to Kaiser. Soon a phone call followed from Franco explaining the conversation Antonio had with one of the goons. Kaiser sat back in his chair and started to write a list of "known" on one side of a ledger and "unknown" on the other. Lois drew a layout of the farmhouse, driveway, barn and the corn field. She penciled in farm roads, told them they had at least one gun and three goons. Then Enrico scratched from memory the Northshore Train Station in Kenosha and said, "I wonder what they're going to do at the station?"

Kaiser said, "So Enrico, you'll be there at the farmhouse. You wait for one or two of them to leave for the pickup and then you go in and get Tony -- that's most important," explained Kaiser.

"Then what?" asked Enrico.

Kaiser added, "Then you deliver a message the goons won't forget. They may get hurt and they all need to disappear. It's your specialty, making goons disappear."

At dusk five Wise Guys drove a black sedan and a utility truck down State Line Road. Then near the farmhouse they turned off State Line onto a farm lane and drove deep into the corn field behind the house. Three Wise Guys made their way through the corn field to within 100 feet of the farmhouse while the remaining two stayed with the car and truck. The Wise guys could hear Tom, O'Brien, and Rizzo arguing about who should have the revolver. Tom insisted he would have it since it was his. Tom then pulled a second revolver he had hidden in a drawer. O'Brien wanted the second revolver while Rizzo wanted it too since he was being left alone with the kid. Finally they agreed to leave Rizzo with the second gun. At 8:00 p.m. two thugs left the house laughing as they walked to Tom's car and drove off.

The Wise Guys waited till the car was well out of sight, then they approached the house. Enrico peered into the downstairs bedroom window and could see Tony gagged and tied to a bed. Enrico went to the front door and drew his gun. Anzalone waited at the front window while Mean Mike went to the back door. Mean Mike knocked to get Rizzo's attention. A startled Rizzo shouted, "Who's there?"

"Your mama!" answered Mean Mike. Just then Enrico busted the front door down and shot Rizzo in the back of his shoulder. Rizzo dropped his revolver as he turned to the back door and saw Mean Mike with a gun. Rizzo was terrified; he panicked and jumped through the front window despite the bullet wound. Just as he hit the ground Anzalone thumped him three times on the head with a club. Mean Mike ran to the bedroom. Tony heard the commotion, but had no clue what was going on. When he saw Mean Mike he started to cry for joy.

Mean Mike gave Tony a huge body hug and told him he was safe. Tony was in tears of happiness all the way to the hidden car while Rizzo was dragged unconscious feet first to the truck bound and gagged and then rolled in a rug.

"I think he got roughed up a bit," said Anzalone.

"The fishes won't care," Enrico said. "Now we go back and wait for the other two, but we got a couple problems. They have a gun and the doors are busted. They'll know something is up. Mike can stay with Tony. We need to keep him safe. Chuck you wait in the truck till the other bums return and then block the road--we don't have much time."

Antonio and Franco drove to the train station with time to spare; they also had two Wise Guys following. Antonio walked to the north end of the boarding platform and waited for the 9:00 Northshore to Milwaukee. Tom was standing only 20 feet away waiting for his chance to grab the cash. Finally the whistle of the train could be heard a long way off breaking some tension. Soon the train's headlight was in plain sight. The train was getting closer and closer. It was at 300 feet, 250, and 200 feet. Tom was thinking, "Put the suitcase down, damn it put the suitcase down." At about 150 feet Antonio put the suitcase down. Tom ran at the suitcase, grabbed it, and jumped the four foot drop from the platform to the tracks. He hit the tracks and tripped just as the slowing train approached. He regained his footing just in time as the train passed. Tom was out of sight from Antonio's view as he finished his run across two more sets of tracks, through a field and then to his brother waiting in his car. His fear turned to joy when he opened the suitcase in the speeding car. Antonio, Franco and the Wise Guys were astonished at what had happened. It was a sly move -- now the train blocked the goons from view and the closest cross street was obstructed by the train so they could not be pursued.

Tom and O'Brien were laughing like school boys all the way back to the farmhouse. "You see, what did I say, no problem with this gig because I laid it out," Tom said. Tom and his brother pulled in behind the farmhouse in the dark. Then the two, still laughing, walked to the farmhouse.

As they approached Tom noticed the back door was damaged and yelled, "Ned it's a trap, run." The two hoodlums turned and ran just as a truck pulled into the driveway and blocked their car in. Several shots were fired from the approaching truck. When the headlights of the approaching truck hit the goons Enrico shouted, "Drop the suitcase and hit the ground." Tom tried to pull his .38 when Chuck clubbed him from behind as the unarmed O'Brien raised his hands. Enrico walked to Tom, picked him up and proceeded to beat him with his fists. When Tom was near unconsciousness Enrico stopped.

While Tom was being beaten O'Brien shouted, "We weren't going to hurt the kid, we wouldn't have!" O'Brien never finished talking because he was then slugged by Enrico several times then tied and gagged. As O'Brien lay on the ground he looked to Tom's eyes as if to say, "Rizzo was right." The two goons were rolled into rugs and loaded into the bed of the waiting truck.

Kenosha Harbor was always poorly lit at night. A black sedan and the utility truck pulled up to the Polansky Commercial Fishing dock. A 27-foot commercial fishing boat was running. Four Wise Guys got out of the sedan and truck and retrieved three large rolled rugs. Although the rolled rugs were tied two were still flailing as they were carried to the boat and thrown into the back stowage area bouncing hard onto the deck. Anzalone was heard to say, "These are expensive rugs for such cheap chumps." There the rolled rugs lay side by side, the two previously moving were now still.

As the boat pulled out of the harbor a large tow chain was wrapped around each rug and locked. When the lights of Kenosha were barely visible the rugs were lobbed into Lake Michigan. After the last rug was dumped Enrico rubbed his bruised knuckles and said, "They will be at peace sleeping with the fishes."

The Pontillos were waiting with great anxiety when the front door bell rang. Roberto shouted, "I got it."

He opened the door and it was Alvano. Alvano had a smile on his face as he walked into the room and asked, "Antonio, have you had any more phone calls?"

Antonio responded, "No!"

Alvano replied, "*Buono* I took care of your problem." Alvano stepped aside and there was Tony, bruised and cut, yet otherwise in good spirits.

The Pontillo house never knew such joy. After hugging Tony, Antonio said, "*Gracia* from the bottom of my heart. Vito get Don Alvano a bottle of *vino*."

Alvano stepped out the door and bid the family goodbye and while lifting his bottle of *vino* in gratitude concluded with, "*Gracia* Antonio, I shall see you soon, but I may call upon you soon for an unquestioned favor."

"*Si*," responded Antonio. He turned to his family and said, "Remember you can trust only family and close friends."

CHAPTER 7

What's In the Barn?

The rough rumble of a truck engine could be heard in the late night darkness of February, 1930. It was now a familiar sound on Monday and Friday nights coming from the Pontillo driveway leading to the barn. Several weeks earlier Enrico had a business visit with Antonio. Enrico had found Antonio sitting in his chair within his grape arbor with his dog Rex at his side. Enrico could smell the aroma of ripe grapes when he greeted Antonio. "*Buon pomeriggio* Antonio. I've come to you with a business deal that I think you will find favorable."

"*Si*," responded Antonio, "I'm listening."

Enrico continued, "Don Alvano would like to make you a business offer. He is in need of a place to temporarily store goods and your barn would serve well. From time to time a truck or two may unload or load goods from the barn in the evening. If you have issues with a neighbor or the authorities let us know, otherwise that is all you need to know. Also, Antonio do you have a milk chute?"

Antonio stood up from his chair pointed to his driveway and said, "*Si* on the driveway side of the house."

"When is your milk delivered?" asked Enrico.

"Monday and Friday," Antonio said.

"If you agree to this offer, then on the second or third Tuesday of every month check the box for your rental payment for the use of your barn."

"See to it none of your family or neighbors become too curious," explained Enrico.

"*Buono*, I could not refuse Don Alvano for all he has done. The barn will be locked," answered Antonio.

Enrico then told Antonio that Don Alvano would be pleased and to have a good afternoon. Antonio was more than happy to help the Don with something so simple and his payment would be in cash. Antonio took a drink of his *vino* and contemplated his garden while Rex lay back down at his feet.

Picture 3. "Don Alvano would like to make you a business offer. He is in need of a place to store goods and your barn would serve well. From time to time a truck or two may unload or load goods from the barn in the evening."

"I wonder what's in those trucks that come and go from the barn," questioned Tony.

"I'm curious too. Who knows around here; besides Nanu said to stay away," responded Vito. "Gwen said her mother wondered what was going on over here, but her dad told their family it was none of their business. It could only be trouble to ask or even to know. Let's get back to sleep. We got school to worry about, especially you, you can do better." The boys could hear the last truck of the week slowly pull out of the driveway and drive north.

Several more weeks passed by with the Cosenza brothers focusing on school and sports. Both were showing a steady improvement in grades: Vito was very organized and was doing well in math while Tony had good grades for the effort he put in. The walk home from school was routine, with Vito and Gwen waiting for Tony, and the three were usually accompanied by two or three others from the neighborhood. There was the usual kids' chatter on the way home. The small group stood at a corner waiting for the crossing guard, a town cop by the name of Pete.

"My dad said all Italians belong to the Mob—is that true Vito?" asked Carter Mohr as he stood waiting.

"Just some of us," said Tony.

"Tony you are not in the Mob and neither is our family," reassured Vito.

"Then what's with the trucks at night?" asked the inquisitive Carter.

"What trucks?" answered Vito, trying to play dumb.

"Let's go kids, the traffic is waiting," shouted Pete the cop.

Curiosity was building within the Cosenza brothers. It was 1931 a year after the start of the barn deal, and the brothers still wondered just what was in the barn: beer, molasses, whiskey, rum? There was only one way to find out. "Here comes another truck," whispered Tony.

"I wonder what is in the barn tonight and what those trucks are hauling," responded Vito. "There is one way to find out and I think I know a way of getting in without anyone knowing the difference."

An excited Tony asked, "What's your plan Vito?" Vito had been thinking for the past two weeks about how to get in the barn. All the doors had padlocks on them except one, the door to the hay loft on the second floor in the back. Vito had been keeping track of what nights the trucks came in and the least activity was Sunday night. All they needed was a ladder.

Curiosity got the better of the Cosenza brothers. On a chilly Sunday evening in October the boys decided they would wait till everyone was asleep and visit the barn. "We don't have a ladder, but Ruffalo has one back by his shop," said Vito. The boys snuck through the alley to Ruffalo's yard and carried his ladder to the back of the barn. They paused momentarily to look at their pa's car parked in the grove of trees near the barn. Vito led the way up first and slid the loft door open, and Tony followed. After sliding the door shut they pulled a light chain to illuminate the loft, allowing them to explore.

Visits to the barn became more frequent. They eventually found barrels of beer and large bags of hops, dry malt, and crushed grains. Boxes marked Corn were actually packed with Canadian whiskey, and they found boxes marked canned meat. What could that be, was it really meat? Upon opening a box they found it was . . . canned meat. The hay loft was packed with stuff for making beer. Occasionally a truck was stored there with keys in the door. Sneaking into the barn became a game of chance that continued through fall, ending when the snow fell. Only once was the barn visited by truckers while they were exploring. The most excitement came when they returned the ladder and crept to their beds undetected.

By June of 1931 the exploration of items being delivered to and transported out became routine, although the boys still got a rush of excitement during their investigations. One time they forgot to close the loft door at night, only to close it during daylight without being seen.

"Nothing new in this truck, just more barrels of beer and a bunch of big blankets," whispered Vito as he pulled away a curtain, shielding the truck contents from casual view. Vito shined his flashlight to see if there was anything they missed in the back. This particular truck resembled an old Conestoga wagon and was marked Lorenzo Bakery. The low sound of their talking was interrupted when they heard a truck pull up and soon after they could hear voices. "Let's hide in the front behind the bench seat," ordered Vito. The boys scrambled to the front of the truck by the large blankets just as the barn door opened. The boys rolled up in the two lower blankets leaving one on top and were motionless.

"Load this truck with two rows of canned meat across the back and then you make the delivery to the East Side Ice House in St. Paul," informed the first driver.

"Got it. That's a long haul and we'd freeze our ass without the blankets up front," replied the second. Within seconds a row of boxes, four feet high, blocked the view of the barrels of beer. The tail gate to the truck was shut, the curtain lowered. The truck was soon rolling down the driveway. The second truck followed the first as it headed down the driveway. The first truck drove south and the second north. The two stowaways didn't have a clue to the location of the East Side Ice House, yet they sure knew of St. Paul and that it was at the end of the Route of the 400. The Route of the 400 was a legendary route of a Chicago and Northwestern passenger train that many said averaged a mile a minute.

The Cosenza brothers were stuck in the moving truck; do they reveal themselves or wait in hiding? One thing was certain, they were very nervous and could hear the drivers' chatter and obscene language as if they were riding on the front seat with them. Most of the talk was of women and how and where to pick up broads.

"Grab me a blanket will you," asked one driver.

"Sure thing," answered the second as he reached for a blanket without looking.

After six hours of driving rough roads and two stops to refuel, a voice said, "Let's stop at the McCormick farm." Vito and Tony never had a chance to escape during refueling stops, because one driver always stood watch. A few minutes later, the truck pulled onto a long driveway and then into a large barn. The two drivers got out of the truck and closed the barn door. It was obvious to the riders where they were. They could smell the heavy stench of cow manure.

When it seemed safe the boys climbed out of their hiding spot and cautiously approached the front barn door. The sun was rising as they peered out a crack. They saw a large farmhouse, acres of pasture, dozens of cows, and a perimeter of what appeared to be endless woods. The brothers had a decision to make. "What now Vito, should we run for it?" asked Tony.

Vito looked around the inside of the barn and examined each door. He discovered they were locked in. There was no escape and he said, "No not now. Keep watch, this door is locked so we can't get out of here without causing a stir. I'll get us some canned meat and we'll find water, even if it is stock water, then we'll decide what to do." The brothers feasted on the meat and found water to drink. Vito thought their situation through and said, "We don't know where the hell we are. If we leave we may be stuck in the boonies for a long time. We stay on the truck until we get back to civilization."

Within a few minutes the boys heard voices; it was the farm family. An older man could be heard shouting instructions to two young boys and a girl. The brothers got back in the truck and concealed themselves once again. For the rest of the day they heard cows mooing, chickens cackling and pigs squealing, but no-one came in the barn.

Vito raised an arm and brought his shirt sleeve to his nose. "Crap, I'm lucky I'm not seeing Gwen—tonight I really smell bad. I smell like the inside of this barn."

Two hours before nightfall the drivers returned and started on their journey. Several hours into the rough ride, Vito felt a tickle in his nose. Then he felt he would sneeze, he held it back. He pinched his nose and held the sneeze once and then twice on his third try he couldn't control it and released a muffled snort. "What the hell was that," said one of the drivers.

"Did we hit a pheasant again?" asked the second driver.

"Hell no! Pull over," commanded the first. The driver slammed on the brakes and grabbed his revolver. Something or someone was under the blankets. The man prodded the blankets with the gun and one edge slowly lifted as Vito peered out. "What the hell are you guys doing here?"

The driver started to get rough with Vito when Vito shouted, "I'm Don Alvano's godson!" Vito stammered in his haste to identify himself and explain how their intense curiosity got them in trouble. Both drivers broke into laughter and the gun went back under the seat. "Okay, we'll take you to St. Paul and let a Wise Guy decide how to get you back to Kenosha where I hope someone slaps your ass," responded the second driver. "By the way I'm Ed and this is Butch."

"I'm Vito and this is Tony," explained Vito.

"We're the Cosenza Brothers," said a smiling Tony.

"Hell it sounds like a trapeze family," said Butch as he laughed.

CHAPTER 8

The East Side Ice House

Back in Kenosha the whole Pontillo household was once again in turmoil. Now both boys were missing. This time it was a bigger mystery because they had both disappeared from home and it was a school day. "Now how do we deal with this?" asked Frank.

Within a few hours their neighbor Ruffalo was at their side door and wanted to know why his ladder was at the back of the barn. It didn't take long for the family to figure out what must have happened. Antonio released a deep sigh as he looked at Maria. "Maria, Maria, Maria I love my grandsons and I pray to Jesus they are okay, but what are we to do? Now I must consult with Don Alvano again."

"We got to get to work, but we'll be home early to help, good luck Pa," Roberto said. Maria was on the verge of fainting, but her tears kept her conscious.

The East Side Ice House looked like an abandoned building from a distance. The street leading to it was seldom used and dark when the Lorenzo Bakery truck arrived. The lights of the truck flashed three times, paused three seconds and flashed three times again. The doors to the ice house opened, the truck entered and the doors were closed. Half a dozen attendants stood by and two more trucks parked in front of a wall of large blocks of ice meant for ice boxes. Vito and Tony felt relieved that someone would likely whisk them home soon. "You boys wait here while we check things out," Butch said. The boys waited. The ice house was chilly and the floor was covered with sawdust giving it an appealing wood odor. The boys could see three men in suits who appeared to be the Wise Guys Ed had spoken of. Ed was animated in his talking with the Wise Guys and they began to laugh.

Picture 4. The East Side Ice House looked like an abandoned building from a distance. The street leading to it was seldom used and dark when the Lorenzo Bakery truck arrived.

There was a loud crash: a truck with a steel wedge in front plowed through the closed doors of the ice house. The truck headed toward the Wise Guys and gunfire erupted. "Get down and stay with me Tony, stay with me," shouted Vito. Bullets flew all over the place and the burrrr of two Thompson submachine guns could be heard. One man tried to climb a ladder and was gunned down. A second ran to the back of the room with

Federal Agents in pursuit. "Let's go," said Vito as he snatched the revolver from under the seat and then grabbed Tony. The boys waited at the back of the truck, twenty feet away from the ice house side door. Bullets shattered glass to an office that a Wise Guy ran into. Stray bullets struck the driver side door of the truck that took them to St. Paul. Two Federal Agents took cover just as a third Wise Guy was shot dead. He lay in a pool of blood just feet from the man who was shot climbing the ladder. The survivors were rounded up and backed up against the wall of ice blocks. Out of sight of the brothers, two agents were still pursuing the third Wise Guy. Ed shouted, "Our hands are up, we're just drivers don't shoot, don't shoot."

Vito whispered, "Here's our chance -- follow me." He grabbed Tony and pulled him along as the boys ran to the side door, opened it quickly and found themselves on a dark side street. They ran as fast as they could and took refuge in a thickly wooded area adjacent to railroad tracks. Within minutes they could hear sirens of State Police, local police and an ambulance. Then there was more gunfire.

"Holy shit," whispered Tony, "I hope this isn't our fault."

"Are you kidding?" said Vito. "That raid was planned days ago. So I don't think so. If we ever get home we are in for an ass kicking. Let's get going before someone sees us or thinks we're involved. I know we're near St. Paul so we need to find the tracks for the Chicago and Northwestern 400 route. They'll lead us home."

CHAPTER 9

Route of the 400

The Cosenza brothers walked the tracks for miles before seeing lights ahead. The boys stopped. "I think it's a hobo camp," said Vito. "We should be okay there for a while. We'll be able to find out exactly where we are." The boys cautiously approached the camp with its stench of burning rubber. Barrels of burning trash and tires could be seen. Cardboard and plywood lean-tos sheltered a small group of colored men singing the blues, while a white guy accompanied them on a harmonica.

The brothers paused for a moment. The music sounded professional and for a second they forgot their objective, but soon continued to the main gathering. Dozens of unshaven men in tattered clothing and worn shoes stood by.

The brothers had never seen such human despair and their relatively clean clothes became an attraction. A medium statured man with a grizzled beard, long dirty hair and filthy clothes said, "So who are you guys, runaways? Nice clothes and new shoes!"

"No we're lost," answered Tony.

Before Tony could finish, a second destitute man said, "Lay off them Rich, it's none of your business." He continued, "Boys this is no place for you. Some of these guys are tramps and can't be trusted and Rich is one of them. You should move on."

"We will," said Vito. "We need to know what line this is. We're looking for the Chicago and Northwestern tracks. You know the 400, the passenger train that goes 400 miles from Chicago to St. Paul!"

"You're on the south side of St. Paul, but on the wrong tracks. These are the Milwaukee Road—follow these south and they'll cross with the Northwestern and they will get you within a few miles of St. Paul Union Station where the 400 stops," answered the second hobo.

"Thanks," Vito replied. The brothers continued in the dark down the tracks. From time to time they would look behind themselves to make certain they weren't being followed.

A few hundred feet down the tracks Tony said, "I didn't like that Rich guy. He was looking at my shoes awful hard."

Vito returned, "He was bad news for sure. We can take a break soon and then head to the 400 tracks."

To their surprise, Rich was waiting in the moonlight at the first trestle bridge. He shouted, "You boys didn't know about the short cut did you? But I did! I've been riding the rails for years and I know all the short cuts." Rich drew a knife and said, "Give me your shoes, kid, and you won't get hurt." Rich switched the knife menacingly from hand to hand and walked toward the boys.

"Drop the knife Rich and get the hell out of our way or I'll blow your face off," commanded Vito as he quickly drew the revolver from his trousers.

"You really scare me," said Rich. Rich walked closer holding the knife in his right hand. He was foolishly thinking—a young kid wouldn't shoot a man over a pair of shoes. But they weren't just any shoes, they were Tony's shoes. A hardened Vito aimed for Rich's chest and jerked the trigger; the bullet struck Rich in the right shoulder. Rich dropped the knife and fell to the track screaming in pain. Blood was flowing through the hole in his shirt. Tony grabbed the knife from the rail tie so Rich couldn't use it in desperation. It didn't matter because Rich slipped off the edge of the bridge falling 20 feet into a river.

Picture 5. The 400 – the Chicago and Northwestern Railroads' famed passenger train and route from Chicago to St. Paul was designated the 400 in 1935. Photo courtesy of the Chicago and Northwestern Historical Society.

"Holy shit," shouted Tony. The brothers ran the rest of the distance across the trestle nearly falling several times. They finally reached the underpass with the Chicago and Northwestern crossing the Milwaukee Road from above. They climbed a hillside to the elevated tracks, slipping occasionally on the tall wet grass. But they were not going to St. Paul; instead they headed east to Wisconsin. An hour more of hard hiking and they approached another long trestle bridge crossing the Mississippi River. Four sets of track crossed the trestle and the furthest track to their left started vibrating and soon the whole bridge began to feel the tremor of an approaching train. Within minutes a freight train was in sight and roared dangerously close by them. Another hour passed by and the sun started to rise.

The Cosenza brothers completed their hazardous hike across the trestle that led them into Wisconsin. Just as they reached the end of the trestle the sky to the west turned an ominous dark yellow. Within seconds a crack of lightning lit the sky. Five seconds later came the roar of thunder. "Oh crap, a storm is moving in from the west. We need to pick up our pace and find shelter or we'll be toasted out in the open like this," cautioned Vito.

"It's just going from bad to worse for us Vito. Look at my shoes. Three weeks ago they were new. Now they look so worn I'll get scolded for that too," groused Tony.

"Well at least you still have them on your feet," replied Vito. "Look Tony," shouted Vito. "A creek! There'll be a culvert to wait in until the storm passes." Just then another lighting shot was followed two seconds later by thunder. A light drizzle soon turned into a downpour. The brothers waited in the culvert, in ankle deep water, for hours before they continued on their trek. Often, they rested from their stressful journey and talked.

"Vito, do you think we should have helped Rich back there?"

"Nope, definitely not," answered Vito. "We could have been killed trying to help him. He made his own decision. Besides, who is that dumb to come with a knife against a gun?"

Back at home, Don Alvano leaned back in his chair and looked at Antonio. He shook his head and said, "Antonio how is it that you are blessed with such adventurous grandchildren? Who in your family do they take after? No, do not answer, I think I know. I will send the word out to search for your grandsons. Somehow I think they will be fine. When all of this is over we need to talk about our arrangement. I was told till now all was satisfactory." Not long afterward Alvano was informed of the raid on the East Side Ice House and three Wise Guys were dead and the drivers and ice house workers were jailed. There was no mention of the Cosenza brothers. Within a short time Kaiser and Enrico were waiting at the Wells Street terminal for the next 400 to Minneapolis St. Paul to investigate the situation and status of the drivers.

The brothers continued on foot for the rest of the day, having only a can of meat to eat that Tony had tucked away. At dusk they spotted a farmhouse a few hundred yards off the tracks. "We are in deep trouble Tony and it may get worse from here," an exhausted Vito said.

"Vito, I'm hungry and my feet have blisters," responded Tony.

"We'll hit the farmhouse tonight. Let's hope they don't have a dog," said Vito. A radio played in the house. At 8:00 p.m. the radio was turned off and two adults and three youngsters stepped out of the house, loaded into a Ford Model T and drove out the driveway to the main county road.

The boys ran to the house and found the back door unlocked. As they entered the house they heard a vicious growl. It was a huge Chesapeake retriever. Vito nervously said, "Hi puppy." The Chessy started wagging its tail as if he were an old buddy.

"Crap," shouted Tony. "The car is coming back."

"Hide," shouted Vito.

"Where?" Tony said.

"The living room behind the couch," said Vito. The boys hid still as they could be with the dog sitting nearby. The back door opened.

"We left the house unlocked. Now where is the box?" said the woman.

"Next to the ice box, Mom," answered a young girl.

"Here it is. Let's go and this time I'll lock the door." The two walked out the door, locked it and were back off in the car. The raid was back on: the boys stuffed themselves on fresh bread, homemade jam and found salted pork and cheese in the ice box. They loaded a carpet bag with canned goods and a knife. Tony threw a chunk of cheese to the Chessy and out they went, locking the door.

"Look Vito a truck," shouted Tony. The brothers boarded the farm truck; a 1927 Ford TT loaded with green tobacco leaves.

Vito pressed the starter, shifted and pushed the spark advance and down the road they went. "We got half a tank of gas and I got 50 cents for more," Vito said. After a few minutes they reached Hudson, Wisconsin, and a paved road and took a right to Eau Clair.

On the outskirts of Hudson they stopped at a service station where they spent the only money they had on gas.

"You boys look too young to be driving, aren't you?" questioned the service station attendant.

"What's too young? I'm 20 and my friend is 17. My pa sent us out to deliver some tobacco," said Vito.

The attendant laughed and said, "Ya and I am President Hoover. I think I better call the sheriff -- you stay here."

In a matter of seconds the brothers were on their way back down the highway as fast as the truck could take them.

On their way to Eau Clair they passed a sheriff's deputy. The deputy slammed on his brakes and did a four-wheel drift, sliding into a creek that ran parallel to the highway. He was stuck. "Slow down Vito. If I die I don't want to be on this highway," yelled Tony. Vito slowed down only when the dust from a vehicle in front began to choke them. The brothers continued driving and watched for the sheriff.

They drove a few more hours through the night before running low on fuel. Vito laid the revolver on the seat and Tony stared at it with his arms folded. "I wonder if Rich the tramp drowned back there," quizzed Tony.

There was dead silence except for the noise of the tires rolling on the highway and the rumble of the Ford engine. Then Vito said, "I don't know, but we ain't cut up are we? I don't care for people like him, and this gun was an equalizer."

"Good afternoon officer." The main jailer at the Washington County Jail had his first visitor of the afternoon. "My name is Alex Kaiser and I am the counselor for Edward Ryan and George Mueller and this is my associate Enrico Parillo."

"Ya, so what," growled the jailer.

Kaiser came back, "Officer, you understand by law my clients are entitled and I said entitled to counsel."

"Okay, okay, but your buddy stays here." Then he shouted, "Bud, bring the dressed up guy to the interview room." The jailer stared at Enrico and went back to reading his paper and smoking a cigarette. Enrico was sitting in a chair when the jailer looked again at him and said, "Paper says the Feds had a raid last night. Are those goons some of them?" Enrico said nothing. The jailer put the cigarette to his mouth and started coughing and said very softly, "I got to quit someday," and went back to reading the paper.

Within half an hour Kaiser had all the information he needed. Kaiser got the two drivers out on bail and then he could have charges dropped. After all they had no weapons and were hired off the street to deliver canned meat to The East Side Ice House. How could they know they were delivering beer? Further, if they kept their mouths shut the Don would take care of their families. The bad news was neither driver knew the whereabouts of the boys, but said the boys had been in the truck.

Tony had fallen asleep while Vito drove through the remainder of the night. "Look," shouted Vito, "a sign; two miles to Eau Clair. We need to ditch the truck. Besides we're low on gas. If we head south we'll run into the Chicago and Northwestern tracks." The boys turned south on the first county road and within a mile came to the tracks. Vito said, "Okay Tony this is what we do. We wrap tobacco leaves around our shoes so dogs can't smell us, then we walk down the creek as far as we can without losing sight of the tracks." The brothers ditched the truck in a corn field, wrapped their shoes and followed the creek for a half mile before coming to a hobo camp. This time the brothers looked the part including the smell. Vito hid the revolver and the boys took a long break. At night they would board a freight train and head south.

"Roberto, I have received word from Franco that Vito and Tony were on a truck that delivered goods to an ice house in St. Paul," said Antonio. "There was serious trouble and some men were killed by Federal Agents and Vito and Tony must have escaped. I want you and Frank to go to St Paul and see if you can find our boys."

"Sure Pa, we'll go right away," responded Roberto.

Antonio finished with, *"Mama mia,* these boys are a driving me a craze, but we are all they have."

After another rest, the Cosenza brothers eased their way to the hobo camp to see about hopping a freight train. To their surprise, a few young boys were in the camp, some with dads and some alone. This too was a destitute bunch that talked of work, losing farms, President Hoover, Black Tuesday, and the Depression.

"Why, I would even work for a Chicago bootlegger," said a former Oklahoma farmer. "I've already lost everything because all I have left is my soul and that ain't worth crap."

The brothers understood now how fortunate they were with most of their family working, even their mother. Vito eased open their bag of food and began eating. At least a dozen pairs of eyes started watching. Vito tore the loaf of bread in half, stuffed the remainder in the carpet bag and tossed it to the onlookers.

The brothers ate the salt pork and bread while the bag was ravaged, as if by a pack of dogs. Vito asked, "Anyone heading south tonight on a freight?"

"I am," said three in unison. "There's a freighter that comes a half hour after the 400. The 400 is always on time and it comes through at 7:40 tonight," said one hobo with confidence.

"We'll be on the freighter too," said Vito.

Tony was trying to remove a sliver of salted pork from between his teeth when he asked, "Is it easy to get on?"

"Does the kid always talk with his fingers in his mouth?" asked the confident hobo.

"No," answered Vito. "So is it hard to get on?"

"Well it's like this. The freight train stops to load potatoes for the Chicago Potato Yard and a few cars of beans are usually loaded first." He paused. "Then the cars are inspected by railroad guards and sometimes detectives, and after the inspections, then we get on." It sounded easy enough as Vito contemplated completing their journey home.

The 400 was on time, stopping briefly to off-load and load passengers. Soon the freight train came in, stopping for additional cars: boxcar, after boxcar, loaded with potatoes, were added to the freight train. The Cosenza brothers couldn't imagine that many potatoes in the world; it was as if the whole state of Wisconsin was growing spuds. Just as the last series of cars were added, four railroad security guards followed their routine of checking above, below and inside cars. The lead guard waved to the engineer and the freight train started to roll just as a dozen hobos and the Cosenza brothers ran for the cars. Vito and Tony and several hobos climbed to the top of a boxcar and were spotted by a guard. The guard was about 100 feet away from the train. The guard ran, yelled, and caught up to the train. He was keeping pace with the train as he ran alongside. He reached out to grab a rung on a ladder, so he could climb on the car, but slipped. He fell alongside the car and before he could get his balance a wheel ran over his left arm. He screamed just as the car severed his arm. The brothers were sickened at the sight.

The band of rail riders found a half full boxcar to conceal themselves in. The riders relaxed as the train built up speed. "I hope I can find work in the stock yards," said a Kansas farmer. Another wondered if he should have gone west to Washington to pick apples or to California to pick peaches.

"I would work a week just to eat a good home cooked meal," said another.

"Me, I could eat three plates of spaghetti and a dozen meat balls," added Tony. Vito then told Tony to get some sleep -- the day was not done. "I miss Pa," whispered Tony.

"I do too," Vito said.

"Vito, did you ever wonder about the meaning of life?" asked Tony.

"Whoa Tony, what made you think of that?"

"I don't know, one day we have Pa and then he is gone. Then I'm kidnapped, that train guard just doing his job and all the rest," answered Tony. "All these guys that were working hard, lost everything, and now look at them."

The freight train continued south. It was scheduled to be in Chicago's Potato Yard by 10:30 that morning, but at least two riders would be off before then. The clackity-clack rhythm of the wheels, passing over rail joints, nearly put the brothers to sleep.

"Guys, everyone wake up, wake up," a voice shouted. The shouting startled Vito and Tony from their sleep. The hobo began instructing, "Listen, our next stop is Wyeville. That guard back there in Eau Clair may be dead, regardless this train will stop and every inch will be searched. We have to bail out as soon as the train slows down, hide and then then get on the next train or get the hell out of here. Those railroad guards will be pissed." Wyeville was just coming into sight when one by one the rail riders jumped off and hid in the brush. They could barely see with limited light. A dozen railroad guards, detectives and sheriff deputies were waiting when the train stopped. Gunfire sounded and cops were chasing hobos.

Four hours later a south bound freight train rolled in. The train slowed enough for the group to get on. It continued to Chicago slowing down for each town it passed through: Adams, Beaver Dam, Milwaukee, Racine, and then Kenosha.

It was 9:45 a. m. when the freight train slowly passed through Kenosha. The boys prepared themselves as the train slowed near the first major intersection. The boys wished the others the best of luck and at 55th Avenue they jumped rolling into tall grass. Other than a few bumps and bruises they were fine. "Let's go Vito," said a panting Tony.

"Wait, I dropped the revolver," said Vito. A few moments later Vito found it and they were on the run in fear they would be spotted: through alleys and between houses and garages to 22nd Street.

"Ma, Nanu, Nana we're okay," shouted Vito as they entered the side door. The brothers were exhausted. It had been more adventure and drama than they expected for just wanting to see what was in the barn.

"Oh my God," shouted Rose as she cried seeing the condition of the brothers. The jubilation was as intense and emotional as it was for the return of Tony.

"There is plenty for you to explain, but first go clean up," said Antonio.

The boys scrambled to the attic where Vito hid the revolver under the floor boards. Vito then turned to Tony and whispered, "I will tell the story, there won't be any mention of the revolver, the shooting or knife, the farmhouse, or truck, train or guard understand?"

"Yes, if we do it will be the end of us and we are already in enough trouble," said Tony. The explanation and story and answers to questions went exceptionally well. Vito explained they hitchhiked and rode two different trucks home. That same night the Pontillo brothers returned home.

"Maria, I have never laid a hand on my two grandsons and I never will. I will leave the discipline to you," Antonio said.

"*Si*," answered Maria. "I will take care of it now." A few moments later Maria was in the attic bedroom with a strap. She was visibly upset.

"Ma, it's my fault, please don't blame Tony for any of this," pleaded Vito.

Maria then shouted, "Do you understand the heartache, stress and embarrassment you two have put on all of us. You could have been *morta*, we know where you ended up and what happened in the Ice House. People were killed! You were irresponsible and you will both be punished first with the strap and then you will not leave this house except for church and school for the next month."

The brothers were happy to be at home, and on their own cots. Sleep should have come easily, but it didn't. Vito had a recurring nightmare of the railroad guard; or he would wake up and think of the hobo screaming after being shot. Over and over, he saw the guard's severed arm and the blood flowing from it.

Saturday evening Vito and Tony walked with their family to Holy Sacrament Church for Confession. Vito and Tony each explained the trouble they had caused. All that needed to be done was for the boys to apologize to Alvano. The boys said their prayers, went to bed and were nearly asleep when Tony said, "Do you suppose the trucks are still going to be coming to the barn?"

"Tony, stop, forget the trucks. You need your sleep."

The business deal with Alvano was still on. From time to time trucks were still moving to and from the barn. An envelope with $50 cash was placed monthly in the milk chute.

Maria told the Cosenza brothers to either get jobs or burn energy on sports, they had no choice. Vito decided to play football again and take a part-time job working for Nunzio the baker and "Big Tony" took up boxing and got exceptionally good. The brothers were expected to spend more time on school work too. Vito and Gwen also began seeing more of each other despite objections from both families. Each encounter became more passionate.

CHAPTER 10

Vito and the Bakery

Job hunting during the Depression was as much work as work itself and if you were a hyphenated American it was harder. Vito looked in newspapers and walked from business to business looking for part-time work. His first stop was a shoe shop where he was disappointed immediately with no prospects at all. After many more stops there was a hardware store that had a sign in the front window, "Part-Time Worker Needed Immediately." Vito stepped in and politely asked about part-time employment. A clerk asked him to wait while he went to the back office.

Vito could hear their discussion, "Excuse me sir, there is an Italian-looking kid asking about the part-time job."

The proprietor peered through a crack in a curtain looking at Vito and said, "They're all gangsters. Tell him we have someone already." Vito continued his search without success until Nunzio's Bakery.

Nunzio had a prosperous bakery and his goods were known as far north as South Milwaukee and south to Zion, Illinois. Nunzio was a recent immigrant, having left Sicily to come to America with his family. He wanted to escape from the Black Hand and experience prosperity. He also employed several people. After three years, he gave everyone a three cent an hour raise. Most bakeries delivered goods by horse-drawn wagons, but Nunzio sold his horses and wagons and purchased two new delivery trucks.

Picture 6. Most bakeries delivered goods by horse-drawn wagons but Nunzio sold his horses and wagons and purchased two new delivery trucks. Circa 1915.

Vito thought he would try Nunzio for a job. He walked into Nunzio's Bakery and instantly was in love with the scent of fresh bread. Vito greeted Nunzio, *"Buongiorno Signor* Nunzio, my name is Vito Cosenza and I am seeking employment."

"You are *Italiano* or *Siciliano*?" asked Nunzio.

"Si, I am *Italiano."*

"Yes of course, Cosenza is in *Italia* and you must be *Calabrese* so you probably think you are smart too! You speak American good: you must have been born here. How old are you and can you drive a truck?" quizzed Nunzio.

"I was born in Kenosha, I'm almost 18, I can drive and I have a license. As for smart I'm good in math," answered Vito.

"Hmmm, can you work Saturday and Sunday very early mornings?" returned Nunzio.

"Yes," answered Vito. "But Sunday I do attend Mass."

Vito was interrupted by Nunzio who said, "You will finish in time for late Mass." He continued, "You'll replace a worthless bum I fired two days ago. He could never make it on time so you must be prompt—and he couldn't count."

"Yes I will be on time and I am excellent in math," answered an elated Vito.

Nunzio was well known for his timeliness for providing fresh baked goods to restaurants and grocery stores. Soon he was baking hot dog buns for several ball parks. To accomplish this he had a night shift of two colored bakers and on Saturday and Sunday mornings, Vito made deliveries with a new truck. Vito was cross-checking his delivery list with a pallet of baked goods to be loaded onto the bakery truck. Just as he was completing the checklist he saw a black Ford Model A race through the alley where he was parked. A moment later there was a huge explosion. He ran down the alley to see where the explosion occurred and five shops south he saw Benedetto's Barber Shop in flames. The fire threatened other buildings and the two new delivery trucks. Vito shouted, "Fire, fire, call the fire department," and then he grabbed keys to both trucks and drove them a safe distance from the flames. The fire department arrived in time to save all except three shops on the block. Police were there too and everyone was interviewed. The police said that an unidentified body was found in the ashes. All Vito could offer was that he had seen a Model A Ford. It passed by too fast to see the occupants or count how many there were.

CHAPTER 11

Prosperity, a Two Edged Sword

Prosperity can sometimes be a two-edged sword and for Nunzio it became a problem. He began gambling on horses and boxing. He brought in a radio and was frequently seen listening to horse races at the Hawthorne track in Chicago. From time to time loan sharks visited him and pieces of papers were exchanged. Over the next two years it went from bad to worse, but Nunzio's business and baking skills still maintained an upper hand on his gambling addiction.

Months after he was hired, Vito was in the back room checking a delivery order when he heard unfamiliar voices coming from Nunzio's office. Vito worked his way through the storage room to within a few feet of the office. He couldn't see inside, yet he knew Nunzio and one of his bakers were in there with at least two others. He could hear the voices clearly now. "It's a shame what happened to your neighbor and his business, it's a too bad things happen—you understand *paisano*?"

"*Si*," answered Nunzio with a shaky voice.

"That's good *paisano*, you are a wise man. You see we can now protect you from such awful things," said the unknown man. One of the men dressed in a grey pinstriped suit walked out of the office and grabbed a sugar doughnut and returned. "We are not violent men, but can keep you safe so we offer you a business deal. We will stop by once a week and you will give us an envelope with say, $25 in it."

The second man then said, "To refuse would cause some bad things to happen. By the way, I see you have a nice wife and three kids—consider them." The two men walked out and took two loaves of Italian bread with them.

Vito walked into the office and it was obvious the two were very shaken. "Vito, say nothing of this and you will live longer than I. I left Sicily do be done with the Black Hand and to find prosperity, then Satan's brothers find me again to squeeze my life."

The following Sunday, Vito noticed a *Chicago Tribune* paper by the cash register on Nunzio's counter. "It's been two years since the Saint Valentine's Day Massacre," said Vito. "I remember there was a huge headline with a description of the Massacre the next day."

"I remember," said Nunzio. "Today's paper said they still can't pin it on Capone."

"Well the Irish and the Italians are still warring, I wonder if Capone was trying to wipe out Moran and his gang?" asked Vito.

"Who knows? They're all *morta*." Nunzio said. "Capone has been trying to take all of Chicago. It's 1931 and there is no peace and I still have to deal with barbarians." Nunzio looked at Vito and noticed his demeanor had changed. "Vito, you look disturbed. Tell me what is troubling you?"

"The St. Valentine's Day Massacre took place on Clark St. and my pa's auto accident wasn't far from there. The cops didn't even care, they just had his car towed to my nanu's and left it to rust. But someday I'll learn the truth."

"*Si*, the thought would trouble me too. In time you will have just good memories of your pa," Nunzio said.

Each time Vito was paid his wages by Nunzio he would give it all to his nanu just as his uncles, aunt and mother did. A small portion was given back to Vito, as the others, for an allowance. Another year passed and to the family's surprise the Cosenza brothers caused no trouble and grades were good. Vito would graduate from high school in spring 1932 and would take Gwen to their Prom. They also planned on enrolling that fall in the same community college. Antonio decided it was time to buy a second car for the family and especially for his two working sons still at home. A used, but clean Hudson was purchased and it was the talk of the block that the Pontillos had two cars. The barn rental money was a big help. Tony was developing an amateur boxing reputation for being so young. He was going on 16. But his quickness and understanding of the sport were exceptional, and teamed with his fearless attitude, he was almost invincible.

Vito enjoyed working for Nunzio and enjoyed talking with the two colored bakers. Vito had now worked in the bakery with them for several years. He also still enjoyed the scent of freshly baked bread, as if he baked it himself, and took pride in his good work.

Vito was always precise with his inventory and it was noticed by Nunzio. "You do well at your counts and deliveries young Vito," said Nunzio. "How would you like to do my books for the bakery? It would require some time during the week."

"Yes, I would like to do that, but what of the deliveries," replied Vito.

"I am doing well enough to hire another for Saturday and Sunday deliveries," added Nunzio.

"Great, I would like that and I would still have time for my college studies," answered Vito.

"Vito call me Vincenzo from now on," responded Nunzio.

The two colored bakers appreciated just having a job in times of poverty. One of them named Noah described to Vito the persecution and prejudice that coloreds were subject to and how lucky they were to have the means to care for their families. Vito could see that although Italians, Irish, and Polish emigrants were looked down on, it was far worse for coloreds. Vito had respect for his two friends knowing their plight and they were an incentive to study harder. Some day he wanted to ask Gwen for her hand in marriage and he wanted to provide for her and a family with a substantial income.

At work Vito was cross checking the bakery's log for sales and expenses. He could easily see that demand for bakery goods was declining. His bookkeeping was interrupted when he heard familiar voices this time. It was the same two thugs who visited Nunzio from time to time to collect their protection money. Vito heard one say, "We need a little more for our lunch, *capisce paisano.*"

After the thugs left Nunzio approached Vito and said, "Vito, I haven't been a good provider to my family. I've been gambling and losing money."

Vito looked Nunzio in the eyes and said, "*Si*, I thought so. I could see your anguish when a horse of yours didn't show or you picked a boxer that lost. Maybe I can help, but you have to follow my instructions." Nunzio agreed he needed help. Vito laid out a plan for Nunzio that would pay the bakery's expenses, including the protection money, from the earnings and with the remainder Nunzio took an allowance to support his family. All went well at first.

America was growing and there was a new influx of emigrants who flocked to the Midwest. More Germans, Poles, Czechoslovakians, and Bohemians came to earn the American dream, enjoy prosperity, and escape economic suppression in Europe. The Danish came too, perhaps the most ambitious of the new Americans. Many moved to Racine, just north of Kenosha. They became well known for their sweet baked goods: kringle, Danish layer cakes, and Danish pastries. Italian baked goods were once thought second to none, but the new Danish bakeries hit the Italian bakeries like a sledgehammer. Worse yet the Danish bakeries made Italian breads that were as good as if not better than some Italian bakeries. This was all devastating to Nunzio because the Danes had moved into Racine and before long had consumed all the baked good business north to Milwaukee.

Vito was uncomfortable with the bakery situation but he knew he would not be working there much longer. That evening he met Gwen after work for a few hours. "Vito, we'll be graduating soon. What are your plans?" asked Gwen.

"Well let's see, I'd like to buy a big new car or travel to Europe before they destroy it with war. Gwen you know what I have on my mind, it's you and only you, but I need to have a firm job to support you and a family. I'm trying to help Nunzio for now but eventually I'll have to find a better job." Vito put his warm arms around Gwen and gave her a hug and kiss then said, "I need to get you home before your folks' suspect you're with me, but we need to talk about your plans on the way home."

"I think they already know I'm with you," responded Gwen.

CHAPTER 12

Murder Witness

Nunzio was in a trap. He was losing much of his business to the Danes despite following Vito's economic help and his rent and protection pay-offs had increased again. His gambling had ended but his debts were not completely paid off. The thugs had already paid Nunzio two visits this week. Vito heard conversations from his upstairs office loft and prepared for the worst; he carried the revolver from the ice house just in case. On the third visit, raised voices caused the colored bakers to run to Nunzio. The surprised thugs fired four or five shots. Vito grabbed his revolver just as the thugs bolted out of Nunzio's office. The second of the two saw Vito and fired from his hip. Vito returned two shots, hitting the first in the left shoulder. Both thugs left the bakery in a waiting car. Nunzio was shot several times and staggered past Vito, stumbled through the backdoor and fell dead in the alley. Both of the colored bakers lay in a huge pool of blood, but Noah was still alive. "Hang on Noah, I'm getting help, hang on!" shouted Vito.

Police arrived within 10 minutes and an ambulance delivered Noah and the two dead men to Kenosha Hospital. Two detectives entered the bakery and the first thing they noticed was Vito holding a revolver. Then the interrogation of Vito began. The lead detective Michaels, asked Vito where the money was and why he shot Nunzio and the colored men. Vito was astounded: after all, he was the one who called for help. "What are you saying," Vito said, "I'm the one that called for help. Besides I work here."

"Take the WOP to the precinct and book him. We aren't done with him yet," ordered Michaels.

"But I think he is the one that called," offered a uniformed officer, Pete.

"Pete, it's me Vito Cosenza, you know me," shouted Vito.

"Come on Michaels I know this kid. He's a good kid, I'm sure he called. I was at the front desk. I'm the one that took the call." Pete looked at Vito and when Michaels turned his back he whispered, "I'll call your family."

"Butt out Pete and get back to watching your kids cross streets," shouted Michaels. Meanwhile two passersby told Michaels that they had seen two men leave the bakery after they heard shots fired and then enter a waiting car. One was wounded, and the witnesses gave a vague description of him and a good one of the second.

Vito's interrogation was brutal. "Sit in that chair, Cosenza," ordered Michaels. "Now tell me how the till got empty, where's the money, who were the other hoods and why you shot the three bakers?" Vito tried to answer, but was interrupted and called a liar. Several times he was struck on his back with a rubber hose by a second detective.

"Can you ask some appropriate questions like what did the thugs look like, why were they at the bakery and what their escape car looked like?"

"Whoa what are you some kind of college boy? Appropriate is a big word. We'll get the information we need out of you later," growled Michaels. "Get him out of here, it's lunch time."

Vito was shoved into a jail cell and was still stinging from the hose beating he received. "Hey kid what they got you in for, stealing tomatoes?" shouted an inmate followed by laughter. Vito said nothing, just slumped back against the wall of the cell feeling its chill on his back. He could smell the stench from the toilet. Vito was eventually allowed to call home. Maria told him they tried to visit, but he wasn't allowed any visitors. She would find him a lawyer.

The following morning was interrupted with more shouting. "Vito Cosenza, get your ass up," shouted a jailer. Vito jumped to his feet despite the ache to his back and the four other inmates sharing his cell jumped as well. "Sit down you pieces of shit. Get over here Cosenza, I don't want to see your guinea ass in here again."

"I'm out for real?" asked Vito.

"Yes you're out, now move," shouted the jailer. Some City Councilman by the name of Madsen and a lawyer convinced the DA and judge to drop charges. Vito scrambled out of the cell and hustled down the hall between cells.

Vito grabbed the bars on the main entrance gate only to get yelled at again. "You want out of here let go of the gate and step back," shouted a second jailer. Vito stepped backed and the gate opened. Vito was led to the front office and was greeted by two well-dressed men: Alex Kaiser and City Councilman Derek Madsen.

Kaiser turned to Madsen and said, "Thank you Councilman. My boss doesn't live in your district, but we have many friends that do and I'm sure we can be of help in the future."

"Of course," said Madsen as he smiled, "anytime. We are always delighted to help our citizens, especially Italian-Americans."

Kaiser looked to Vito and asked, "How did you like your over-night stay in Kenosha's finest hotel?" Vito didn't answer he just smiled -- he just wanted to get out of the place. Vito was checking through a sack the cops had handed him with his personal belongings when Kaiser said, "You'd like to know Noah will be okay and told police you didn't shoot any of them and that thugs took Nunzio's cash before they killed him. Unfortunately they discounted his testimony at first, I think because he is colored. It's just lucky the two witnesses outside were white."

"I'm relieved to know Noah is okay it's too bad about the others. They were good guys," said Vito. "As for the cops, I don't know whose side they are on!" Kaiser drove Vito home.

Vito had yet another lesson, this time in police brutality and prejudice. He could not understand how the very authority that was to protect and preserve the peace could be the ones that despised citizens. What did it matter if you did business honestly and tried to abide by the laws? What was the difference when one year you can drink a beer and the next you can't just because a minority decides you can't. He reasoned all the Mob was doing was providing to the public what they wanted: alcohol, prostitution and gambling. It was true some were outside of the limits of morality, but so were some cops and politicians.

Once again Vito was greeted at home by most of the Pontillo family. "We tried to help," explained Frank.

"But the *polizio* would not allow us in and were very unfriendly," added Antonio.

"I know, I know Nanu," replied an apologetic Vito. Vito turned to his uncles. "I'm old enough to move out on my own as soon as I find myself another job and I'll graduate soon."

"*Si*," said Roberto, "I'll be moving out in two months too when I marry Luisa."

Several days passed by before Vito had a visit from another detective named Willis. This time the interview was different and started with an apology. Willis and a second detective knocked on the Pontillo door and were greeted by two angry men, Roberto and Frank. "So what do you want?" said a bitter Roberto.

"Look, I'm sorry about what happed to Vito Cosenza, but I would like to talk to him and you can sit by if you like," answered Willis in a civil voice.

"We'll get him, but you come into our home after you treated one of us like scum because we are Italian!" said Frank. Roberto went to the garden to get Vito. Vito walked into the living room where the detectives waited. Willis again apologized for Michaels' behavior, explaining he over-reacted, he was a bigot and had been harshly disciplined for his unprofessional behavior. "I'll say nothing without a counsel present," responded an angry Vito.

"That won't be necessary Vito. You have been totally exonerated by virtue of the testimony of Noah and other witnesses, and we have a document signed by the chief to that effect including an apology to you," said the second detective. Vito was surprised. He explained in detail what he had seen, and the detectives justified his use of the revolver and returned it to him. Willis said Vito's story collaborated with the other witnesses who saw the thugs run from the bakery. They also had a better description of the vehicle. At least one of the thugs used a .45 pistol because spent cartridges were found on the bakery floor. Vito said he could identify the thugs in a line-up if need be.

CHAPTER 13

The Sit Down

One thing was certain: another thank you was due to Alvano for getting Vito out of the slammer. Vito was very familiar with Mafia protocol. He could not go directly to the Don, but would need a second individual.

Vito walked to Franco's home and explained what needed to be done. Franco said he would help with a meeting by finding a Wise Guy to be the intermediary. Vito returned to the Pontillo home and sat at a widow and contemplated his visit with Alvano. Vito could see the barn and in the far corner was his pa's car. He wondered about his pa and the suspicious stories of his accident. Vito's daydreaming was interrupted by the scent of Italian sausage, oregano, and other spices from the dining area, supper was ready.

Franco was greeted by Vito at the Pontillo home and said, "Vito it's arranged." After taking a puff of his cheap cigar Franco said in two days they would drive to Waukegan. There they would meet Enrico and he would escort Vito to Don Alvano's office.

Two days seemed to take forever. Vito had to make up for time lost with his homework so he could graduate on time. He had become somewhat of a celebrity when his friends learned he had wounded one of the thugs and likely saved Noah's life. Vito downplayed his role. After all, he explained, two lives were lost and a third could have been.

Franco drove Vito to Falduto's Italian restaurant in Waukegan where they met Enrico and had lunch. "I love the Italian sausage here--they make their own you know," said a smiling Enrico. After a healthy bite of the sausage Enrico took a large amount of spaghetti on his fork and then took his spoon, placed the spaghetti on the spoon and spun it. Enrico noticed Vito was watching as he spun the spaghetti. He looked at Vito and said, "I look like a Sicilian peasant don't I? Oh, the Don is looking forward to your visit." Enrico took another heap of spaghetti in his mouth and waived his fork toward Vito and said with his mouth full, "There is something about you the Don likes."

At the end of lunch Enrico asked Franco to wait while he and Anzalone drove Vito to Alvano.

"Vito, sit in the back," directed Anzalone. Vito followed instructions and looked for signs of blood, bullet or knife holes and saw none. Vito wondered how many traveled in this car and wound up in Lake Michigan, the sand dunes, or in a Chicago sewer.

Enrico lit an expensive cigar and chuckled as the smoke drifted to the back seat. "Relax Vito. I know what you're thinking. We never whack someone sitting alone in the back seat. I'm joking Vito." Anzalone burst into laughter and Vito smiled. He knew he'd be okay.

Vito was escorted several hundred feet through a courtyard of a modest mansion. Vito had to wait several hours for Alvano. Waiting with him were several well-dressed men. Enrico explained they were body guards for bootleggers. Alvano was in council with their bosses. Alvano didn't like to associate with them because he thought they were close to heathens. He had helped them in the past avoiding all-out wars and strayed from his normal business by helping sell beer and Canadian whiskey. For that Alvano was on the edge as far as some of the other Families were concerned. Alvano also knew who had killed the bakers and warned that nothing was to happen to Vito Cosenza. He liked Vito, but this order was for business reasons.

"Enrico, you and Vito may come," Nick said. Enrico and Vito entered Alvano's office and Vito kissed the back of his hand.

"Don Alvano, I have come to show my indebtedness for my recent event with the police and of course I will never forget the past, your saving my brother Tony."

"For such young men, you and your brother have caused a lot of attention. I think it's due to your fearlessness, curiosity and just being in the wrong place at the wrong time," replied Alvano. Nick smiled and started to laugh, but then held back. "Nick what are you thinking?" asked Alvano.

"I'm impressed with the Cosenza brothers too. They are not only characters, but they have character and are survivors."

"Vito, I understand you are graduating soon with studies in math and business," Alvano said.

"Yes I am," replied Vito.

"You're still young, but there may be a time when I can use your services. I would think that our meeting today would suggest you would respond favorably."

As Vito kissed the back of Alvano's hand he said, "Don Alvano you can count on me."

"*Buono,*" Alvano said. Vito and Franco returned home in time for Vito to secretly take Gwen to a movie.

Due process for the thugs who were squeezing Nunzio was never achieved. They were both rounded up within three weeks and identified by Vito, Noah, and two passersby in a line-up. A trial date was established and the two thugs and driver were out on bail within 24 hours. The day before the trial was to start they were all found floating face down in the Pike River. They had been shot. No one knew anything, including the lawyer who got them out on bail. In an odd way justice still prevailed as far as Nunzio and the colored man's families were concerned.

Before graduating, Vito went job hunting. He preferred to stay in the Kenosha area, but would move to New York, Philadelphia or Boston if a job was offered. Deep down he had always wondered if some day he could join Alvano's Family, but that would have to be in the future. Vito inquired about jobs with several large companies: Case Manufacturing, Nash Automotive, and three banks. He even considered teaching school, but then to his surprise he was offered a job with the Kenosha Branch of the Wisconsin Bank and Trust. The bank officers were impressed with Vito's math skills and his professional business mind. They hired him, despite Vito being Italian.

Vito started out with menial jobs, but soon he had a modest promotion and was working on business loans. At a time when businesses were slow it was important that investments were sound for the bank.

Vito's next step was to rent an apartment on the north side of Waukegan. He was independent of the Pontillos' home and was still close enough to date Gwen. Gwen was working in Kenosha as a teacher's assistant.

CHAPTER 14

Big Tony Moves to Detroit

The bell rang for the third and final round in a smoke-filled gym. It was so dim you could barely see the two fighters in the center of the ring. Until the second to last round it had been an even fight. The last round would decide the winner. At the start of the final round Big Tony had a swollen left eye and a slight cut on the chin while Gonzalez had a broken nose and blood dripping from his ear. Gonzalez threw the first punch, missing with a left jab. Big Tony countered with a right hook over Gonzalez's jab and connected on the forehead, followed by two hard left jabs and a crushing right hook to the jaw. Gonzalez fell-face first-to the mat and his legs quivered as the referee counted him out. Big Tony walked calmly to his corner and was greeted with hysteria while the fans betting on Tony were equally hysterical for their winnings. Big Tony raised his arms not in victory but to acknowledge his fans. He then turned to check on Gonzalez and said, "How is your nose man, you did a beautiful face first on the mat. That must have hurt." Gonzalez was unaware of anything at the moment. Gonzalez had been the best amateur heavyweight in the Chicagoland area and to Tony the match was a stroll through the park.

"What's wrong Tony," asked Mel Thompson, Tony's trainer.

"Mel, these chumps aren't worth my time. A few whacks and they roll over."

"He's got a point," said Dick Kenny, Tony's cut man and assistant trainer.

Big Tony was still raw. After losing his third and fifth fight, he won the rest and was 42 and 2. "We'll talk more," Mel said.

Big Tony had grown to 6' 4" and weighed 235 pounds. His coordination had caught up with his body. His skills and speed were exceptional for his size. Big Tony's managers knew he had outgrown the competition; he still needed a lot of honing. Everyone knew he could not get that in Chicagoland and the best thing to do would be go to Detroit and the world could be his oyster.

"Man does it stink in here. Is it ever cleaned up? I mean this is disgusting Tony," offered Vito.

"Yeah and it can get worse," responded Tony. Tony had just finished sparing and was shoving toilet paper up his nose and had gauze in his mouth to stop the bleeding. Vito had come to the gym on 60th Avenue at Mel's request to talk about Big Tony's future. "Shit," shouted Tony, "I'm still bleeding. What's worse is when I piss blood. I love boxing, but I need to move to get better competition and training facilities."

Mel saw Vito talking to Tony and said, "Hi Vito, are you talking about Tony's future?"

"Yes, but we need to involve his ma too so let's meet with her Tuesday at Demark's during her break."

Demark's Bar was not busy for a Tuesday night. "Hi Mrs. Cosenza, how are you tonight?" asked Mel.

"I'm fine Mel. I'll meet you in the corner booth." Maria pointed in the direction of the booth and said, "Anything to eat or drink?"

"How about: a couple Italian sausage sandwiches and a round of Cokes." Mel asked.

"Sure thing," answered Maria. She knew what was up and that either or both of her boys would move some day. She had known Mel for five years and he could be trusted. To know that Vito would be involved in the decision making was reassuring. Maria came back to the table with their order and a coffee for herself. "Well it's no secret you want to move my Tony, but Vito needs to be involved in any decisions."

A few minutes later Vito arrived and a plan was laid out by Mel. He and Tony would move to Detroit and set up at the First Round Gym near the inner city. He would apply to turn professional and earnings from fights would pay room and board. But they needed $200 up-front money first. "Tony is still a prospect not a contender yet," explained Mel. He would have to win his first 10 fights before he could get meaningful competition. Plenty of "club fighters", who worked days, trained occasionally and were willing to have their head caved in for beer money.

"How long before you know Tony has a future as a contender?" Vito asked.

"Probably two to three years," responded Mel.

"Are there many Italian Restaurants in Detroit?" Maria asked.

"A few--why?" Mel asked.

"Why he needs good Italian food and you can't feed him something like bland German or Polish food and expect him to stay healthy!" quipped Maria.

Mel laughed and said, "Good point, I hadn't thought of that. I'll make sure he gets some Italian food in him."

"Vito, what do you think?" asked Maria.

"There are some important points we haven't discussed. We need a bonded contract with the gym for sufficient training time and use of equipment, and time for sparring partners." Vito went on with many more points and said, "I'd also like to see any existing contracts and review them for consistencies and visit the gym and some of the trainers."

"I thought you were a bookkeeper or something, not a lawyer," responded Mel. He followed up with, "No, that is all fair enough. I'll get on this tomorrow and call my buddy Jack Engram. I've already talked to him about Tony."

CHAPTER 15

Angelo's Car

The rap tap tap knock at the door was distinctly different from the normal tap of the bank's secretarial staff. "Come in," Vito responded. A large modestly dressed and clean shaven man walked in. He spoke with a firm deep voice, "Mr. Cosenza, my name is Eric Wagner and I'd like to talk to you about a bank loan to start up my own service station and I have the appropriate paper work already right here." Wagner held the papers high in his hand for Vito to see.

"Come in and sit down, let's see what you have," Vito said. Vito looked over Wagner's application and asked general questions: what proportion outside of the loan did Wagner have for start-up money, and more. It would be six days before Vito could give Wagner an answer regarding the loan, it looked very positive. "Mr. Wagner please come to my office next Thursday, by then I will have reviewed this with our Loan Board and have an answer to your loan request," explained Vito.

"Thank you," responded Wagner. Vito watched Wagner leave his office and wondered if he could be of help examining his pa's car that was still rusting in the back yard.

Vito followed up with Wagner's loan request with the board and it was approved. After visiting with Vito, Wagner was excited to get his business going. "If there is anything I can do for you Mr. Cosenza please let me know. This is wonderful news," shouted the delighted Wagner.

"As a matter of fact there is, let's take care of all this paper work first and then arrange to discuss what I need over a beer," answered Vito.

"Absolutely," responded Wagner, "A nice cold beer sounds great. Too bad we had wait until 1933 to successfully repeal Prohibition. Now it's 1934 and we can drink cold beer and not worry about the Feds."

"Amen for that," said a smiling Vito. "Let's meet at Demark's Bar here in Kenosha."

Demark's was booming and serving beer legally had improved business 150%. "Hi Ma," said Vito, "this is my friend Eric. We're going to talk business and would like a quiet booth." Maria escorted the two to a booth away from the main door and the restrooms. Vito explained the unusual circumstances his pa had died under. With the car crash and no investigation, it had been assumed he was speeding and he lost control. The car was left to rust near a barn out back near the family home and he wanted Wagner to look at it. The two consumed a few beers and made arrangements to meet that next Saturday.

"Hey there Vito," shouted a deep voice. It was Bruno. "Silly thing, to see a mother serving her son beer in a bar."

"Well, at least it's legal now," followed Vito. Vito watched Bruno Salvatore as he walked to the bar and slushed down a 12 ounce brew. But Vito was uneasy when he noticed Bruno staring at his mom.

"Vito, Vito," whispered Wagner, "I need to get going. I'll see you next Saturday."

"Oh right, I'll see you next Saturday."

Vito stared at his pa's car as if frozen in time: it had been 10 years since his death. The front windshield had a round depression as if hit by an object, the front end was smashed, the passenger door was damaged, but it could open while the passenger window was completely busted. Wagner looked at the vehicle, examining the front and the wind shield. There was just a hint of different paint on the driver's side and it could still be seen on small patches on the side of the front bumper too. "You say there was no investigation?" asked Wagner. He was already very suspicious some very conspicuous clues were ignored.

"None," Vito reported.

"I'm going to crawl underneath and check the undercarriage," said Wagner. Wagner kicked away weeds with his foot and with a knife he cut some brush to make a trail to crawl through. Vito could hardly hear Wagner as he talked to himself while inspecting the joints, cables, hoses and the frame of the neglected car. Vito opened and closed the driver's side door several times when he heard Wagner sliding out from under the car. "Tell me again, what you know about the accident," asked Wagner.

"My pa was apparently parked on Clark Street in Chicago, visiting a friend, and I guess the car was facing slightly downhill. There were no witnesses, but we were told by the cops he pulled out, accelerated and lost control and went down an embankment, hit a tree and then into the Chicago River. He died on the way to a hospital, and that is all we know. All of that is speculation, the cops don't really know," Vito explained.

"Why was he in Chicago?" Wagner asked. "Clark Street is where the St. Valentine's Massacre occurred."

"I don't know how close to the North Side Mob territory his visit took place. We think he was visiting business friends, we really don't know what he did for a living. He provided for us," Vito explained.

Wagner said nothing and reached into the cockpit and pushed the brake pedal: it gave way easily. "Vito, I think your dad's car was sabotaged. The brake lines were cut." Wagner explained that up until a few years before this model and year, cars were equipped with mechanical brakes, but in 1922 hydraulic brakes came out and although they were new engineering they were fairly reliable. Even after all these years it was easy to see that the brake hydraulic hoses had been cut with a knife. "I also think someone sideswiped your dad because the paint on the car doesn't match the paint in the dents to the side."

"Holy shit, sweat Jesus in Heaven, who would do that?" Vito asked. Vito grabbed the end of his mustache and twisted it as the anger built up. He thought he was over his pa's death, but now his mind was racing. What was Pa's business, why was he on Clark Street a known hoodlum neighborhood, and why was his car sabotaged? Vito looked at Wagner, who was visibly nervous when he realized he may have entered a world he had previously wanted no part of.

"Eric, say nothing of this. Your life could be at risk if you do. All along I thought I knew who my pa was and now I'm not sure," Vito explained.

That Saturday Vito walked with his family from the Pontillo home to Holy Sacrament for Confession. Vito's heart was burning with a vendetta.

He had to find the person or persons responsible for his pa's death. He needed to fulfill the vendetta for his family's justice, but felt uneasy because he would be taking at least one life. Vito sat with his family and waited for his turn. When his opportunity came he walked to the booth, slid open a curtain and then closed it. After he knelt and made the sign of the cross he said, "Forgive me Father for I have sinned, my last Confession was two weeks ago."

Father Falbo then replied, "Yes my son. God bless you, continue."

Vito resumed, "Father I have discovered my father was murdered. Someone sabotaged his car and ran him off the road. I must find the one's responsible and bring justice for my family."

Father Falbo became nervous. It was in that same Confessional booth a decade earlier that he had Confession with Angelo. Angelo had always felt he could trust Father Falbo and take his troubles to him. He had committed numerous crimes and wanted to go straight, but felt trapped by his success. Of all people Father Falbo could provide the spiritual support Angelo would need. He confessed to Father Falbo of a jewelry store heist and where he had hid his share of the loot. Angelo was concerned for his life and wanted Father Falbo to turn the loot over to the police if he were killed. Otherwise he and Father Falbo would eventually figure out what the right course of action should be so he wouldn't be incriminated. He didn't want his family implicated either. But after Angelo's death Father Falbo got cold feet and became greedy. At an opportune time he secretly took some of the hidden jewels and pawned enough to buy himself a new car. He justified his action thinking he deserved something nice in life yet he knew it was wrong. He had committed a felony. He just wanted his problem to go away. Father Falbo paused a few moments then asked, "My son that would be a very serious offense of God's Commandment, 'Thou Shalt Not Kill.' Please report this to the authorities."

Vito responded, "Father they have done nothing." Father Falbo was nervous and ended the Confession prematurely, sending Vito with his penance assignment. Vito had resurrected a ghost of guilt in Father Falbo.

Wagner never said a word about his inspection of Angelo Cosenza's car, but he was busy building his service station business. Wagner had exceptional mechanical skills in an age when vehicle improvements were continuously being developed. He was also an excellent businessman and had great customer relations. Before long Wagner was back to the Wisconsin Bank and Trust and meeting with Vito with another business proposal. He entered Vito's office with a nervous smile. "Sit down Eric," Vito said.

Wagner sat and stared at Vito for a moment looked around the room and with his first words he said, "Do you know any more?"

"No," responded Vito, "this will be a very slow process. Now what do you have on your mind, not that I don't already know." Wagner handed Vito a new completed loan form and several affidavits. Vito made a quick review and said, "This looks good, but I can make it better, much better." Vito normally didn't do more than what he was authorized to, but thought this was an important step for Wagner and wanted to help.

"Sure," responded Wagner, "take your time."

Vito looked the documents over, "This will only take a day, but my changes will greatly improve your position with the Loan Board."

Vito's concern about the loss of his pa and the emptiness he and Tony had suffered over the years since his death would never go away. But maybe if he learned the truth it would help. The time was now to start his own probe and he would start with his ma. He thought this evening would be as good a time as ever since it was her night off. Vito was very organized and detailed in his quest to find out why his pa's car was sabotaged. He started by reading old newspapers keeping a log of the events of the day.

Plenty of outlaws were around in the 30s including Ma Barker, Bonnie and Clyde, Dillinger and Baby Face Nelson. Much of their activity was in strong-arm robberies, especially of banks. There was also a gang war going on between the North Side Gang of Irish and the South Side Gang of Al Capone and mainly Italians. Could his pa have somehow been involved with the Mob, in Chicago sometimes called Outfit? If he was, he did a good job of concealing it from the family. Still, why would no one know what he really did other than provide for his family? Vito would talk to others, including his second cousin Mean Mike.

Vito called his mom from his office and after some small talk about his new job he asked if she would have time to talk with him that night. Maria knew what was on Vito's mind and was more than willing to know the truth herself about Angelo's death, since the authorities didn't seem to care. After work he met Maria and they sat and talked in the family's grape arbor. "Ma, what did Pa do for a living," Vito asked.

Maria was surprised by Vito's question and sat up in her seat and looked at him. "I really don't know and I didn't feel it was my place to ask. An Italian wife does not ask a husband what he does for business when he provides for his family as well as your pa."

"Ma, what do you remember about the days before Pa's death?"

"It has been so long ago. I remember he had a phone call and said he'd be gone a few days. He came home and then had to leave again. The next we knew he was killed in a car wreck. He was always so careful," answered Maria. "Oh I forgot," said Maria, "it was the day before that he gave me a pin, like Cupid's bow. I just love it."

"Thanks Ma, we'll figure this out."

She continued, "It was a brand new car Vito. Well, it was used, yet only a year old. He only had it a couple weeks."

Vito thought, I need to check the car's mileage. He only made two trips. The mileage, minus the one way trip to Clark Street would be the approximate distance to his first destination. "Ma who did he buy the car from?"

"He bought it from Snyder's in downtown Kenosha." Vito walked the 300 feet and checked the mileage of his pa's car as it sat in the brush; it had 6,704 miles. Vito found the car's sales receipt in a box where Angelo kept his important papers. The mileage for the car was on the receipt, and simple math suggested his pa's trip was 960 miles round trip or 480 miles one way.

CHAPTER 16

A New Career Opportunity

Roberto and Luisa had a typical Italian wedding with plenty of food, great music, entertainment and dancing. Luisa was Greek and although her parents wanted her to marry within her nationality they were happy she at least married someone with Mediterranean ancestry. The wedding reception was being held at the local Italian American Club with its complement of wedding crashers. "Vito," whispered Mean Mike, "grab Tony and meet me next to the side door. See those three drunks?"

"Yes," said Vito.

Mean Mike continued, "They crashed the wedding and have already consumed $20 in booze and have been rather obnoxious. We're going to escort them out."

"Fine," responded Vito. "I'll get Big Tony and we'll deal with them, but let me handle it." Mean Mike smiled because he had never seen an aggressive Vito except on a football field. The three approached the reception crashers and Vito asked them to step outside and he would explain a deal they had for them.

Surprisingly the three walked out the door followed by the cousins. The biggest of the drunks asked, "So what's the deal smart ass?"

Vito followed with, "Here is the deal. You're not welcome, leave now and you don't get hurt."

The biggest drunk laughed. He was several inches taller than Vito. The drunk said, "Shake," and held out his hand. Vito fell for it and held out his hand. When the drunk put out his hand he said shake and then pushed the point of his fingers into Vito's stomach and shouted, "Spear."

"I get it," responded Vito. He looked at his adversary and said, "Shake." When the drunk put out his hand thinking he was going to get a handshake Vito delivered a blow to his stomach with his fist and said, "Punch." The drunk doubled over from the blow just as Vito smashed the back of his neck with a forearm. Standing him up Vito delivered a blow to the drunk's nose. Vito looked at his bruised knuckles and turned to the two drunks who remained standing; they had lost all confidence in their big buddy. Then Vito said, "Now, I'm going to give you a spelling lesson, B-I-G doesn't spell B-A-D, what do you think?"

One of the two standing drunks said, "I think we have had enough excitement for the day."

"Good," responded Vito, "I don't like giving spelling lessons." The two drunks picked up their unconscious friend by the shoulders and dragged him off.

"Holly shit Vito, what got into you? That was *terrifico*," said a hysterical Mean Mike.

Just then Big Tony added, "He was my best sparring partner." Mean Mike had never seen this side of Vito. He saw an intellectual who had a wit and now a tough guy side.

Vito rejoined Gwen at the Pontillo family table and the two enjoyed the reception ceremonies. Vito took Gwen's hand and led her to the dance floor and put his arm around her waist and then she drew him closer. He looked at her affectionately and said, "Gwen, you are absolutely the most beautiful woman here and for that matter the world!" Antonio over-herd Vito and looked toward Rose with her Irish Fiancé and then toward Gwen and thought, 'She is beautiful and smart and he knew someday he would welcome her and the young Irishman into the Pontillo family. After all, this was America where ethnic purity was rapidly fading.'

Gwen looked into Vito's dark eyes squeezed his hand and pushed her breasts into his chest--and whispered, "I love you."

An hour later Mean Mike approached the Pontillo family table and said, "*Scusare* Vito, can I have a minute with you."

"Sure," replied Vito, "more drunks and reception crashers."

"No, more important," replied Mean Mike. Vito and Mean Mike walked to a rose garden where Mean Mike drew out an expensive cigar and lit it.

"This is serious," said Vito, "Mean Mike, you're going to propose."

Mean Mike smiled and said, "No, but what I have to say is a proposal and confidential. Vito look at me, I'm well dressed, I have money, I have a nice car, and I have women. Vito, you could have all this. The Don wants to bring you into the Family as a business associate. From what I have seen you should be a hit man."

Vito straightened out his own lapel, combed his black wavy hair, and then reached out and straightened Mean Mike's tie. "Tell the Don to arrange a meeting in a month. The bank has been good to me and I want to finish some work before I resign. I would love to join as a business associate."

"*Buono*," said Mean Mike.

Vito immediately injected, "But I have something to talk to you about with extreme confidentiality too, but not now."

"*Si*," responded Mean Mike.

CHAPTER 17

A Chain of Service Stations

"This appears to be an excellent proposal and loan opportunity," explained a member of the Business Loan Board.

"I think so too sir," Vito responded.

"None of us see a problem here, especially in these times when there are plenty of problems," explained the Loan Committee Chairman.

"Good," said Vito, "I'll call Mr. Wagner first thing in the morning."

Wagner was at the door of Vito's office almost simultaneous to Vito's call. This time Wagner was dressed in a business suit and tie, he was hansom and looked like a business man. The big loan was approved for a chain of service stations. Wagner was again excited to be on a new and bigger business venture. "Thank you so much Vito. I know you greatly improved the proposal in ways I had never thought of."

"You're welcome," replied Vito. "I will be leaving the bank in two weeks, but I think we can do business in the future. My new employer has huge financial support."

Vito asked to meet his immediate supervisor and the bank president. He explained he had two important matters to talk about and one was his resignation in two weeks. First Vito explained, he had been researching all of his colleagues' transactions and discovered who the bank embezzler was.

It was an older disgruntled employee who had taken more than $50,000 in bank funds by setting up bogus investments. He showed his managers the books and explained how he had secretly determined how the banker was inserting the bogus accounts and removing money. He then announced his resignation. The bankers were thankful for his service and also appreciated his skillful detective work ferreting out the illegal transactions and the embezzler.

A meeting was soon arranged with Don Alvano. Alvano explained he was well aware of Vito's business skills at the bakery, and the bank. Tough times were upon the Family businesses mainly because of the repeal in Prohibition. Mobsters were still selling beer in the early years following repeal of the Volstead Act. The Cullen–Harrison Act had been signed by President Franklin D. Roosevelt on March 22, 1933. It authorized the sale of 3.2 percent beer and wine, which allowed the first legal beer sales since the beginning of Prohibition on January 16, 1920. Now, Mom and Pop breweries were starting up all over, and some of them were getting big, especially in nearby Milwaukee. Previously they were brewing non-alcoholic beer. This required the Mob to look elsewhere for money-making schemes. "Vito," explained Alvano, "your job will be to discover new business opportunities for the Family. You'll have the full support of the Family and you'll be treated with respect like a *Copo*."

Vito's mind was running wild with schemes he had already thought of, some riskier than others. This was business and he was up to it. Perhaps he wouldn't have been a few years earlier, today he had a whole new outlook on reality. Vito responded, "I'm pleased you have asked me, I will not let the Family down. Now what is the initiation?"

"Vito you are *Italiano* not *Siciliano*, I'll talk to the other members of the Outfit, we have similar blood, but the rules were made for Sicilians, but most of them are *Italiano* too," explained Alvano, "chances are it won't matter."

Within a year Wagner had three more service stations with one each in Zion, Waukegan, and Evanston along with his first in Kenosha. Wagner had plans to build two more as soon as he had his three new stations established. While Wagner was building his business Vito had gone to work for Alvano. Vito's first assignment was to work out business ventures for the Family that would be money makers. For Vito this was an exciting challenge. He had a scheme that he felt was going to be very profitable, but he needed Wagner and other service station owners.

The final fuel storage tank was being placed at Wagner's Waukegan service station. Wagner was overseeing the work when a 1933 Buick drove up nearby and parked. It was Vito Cosenza and he wasn't alone. A well-dressed body guard accompanied him. "Eric it's me Vito. How are you? You look busy!"

"I am, but good thing I'm here because these clowns don't know what they're doing," responded Wagner.

"Eric do you have a minute or two," asked Vito.

"Yes, let's go into the station office," said Wagner. Vito asked his body guard to stay nearby while he and Wagner talked. Vito explained that one of his new businesses was distributing gas and oil to service stations and he would appreciate Wagner's business. He further explained that if he already had contracts he could persuade the other distributor to void the contract. There would be a confidential monetary reward for Wagner if he participated.

"How would you do that?" inquired Wagner.

Vito responded, "Leave that to me. I have ways of persuading people to do the right thing." Vito continued, "As a matter of fact I have a contract here with one of my companies that you can sign today." Wagner was nervous as he looked the document over. "Relax Eric," assured Vito, "there is no risk to you. We sell you the gas or any other petroleum product, you pay cash, you sell the product, you get rewarded and we have to deal with the state and federal tax revenues." Wagner was still nervous, but signed. "Good," said Vito. "You let us know when to deliver. It's very simple. Our trucks will be marked Billings Petroleum Service and we will give you our business address at the first delivery. "Oh by the way," Vito continued, "I want to talk to you later about the new cigarette machines we have. You just stick in a dime and a pack pops out, *presto.*"

Wagner would have five productive service stations, but that wasn't enough. Vito's ambition exceeded that of Alvano's. This ambition was sometimes a concern for those around him. Regardless of Vito's business focus he was still secretly possessed to get to the bottom of what he now considered his pa's murder. He had learned who his pa was working for with the Mob and was rising through the ranks but wanted to venture on his own. There was also the rumor that Mean Mike told him about, that his pa may have been a safe cracker. Yes, there was more to learn.

CHAPTER 18

"Big Tony from Detroit"

Tony took on the fight name of "Big Tony from Detroit." Few knew where he was really from, but it didn't matter because the fight fans loved him, and that he was from Detroit. Tony's fights came quickly at first and as he fought through the chumps the quality of opponents improved, but the rate of fights slowed down. He had compiled a record of 6 and 0. Heavyweights like Gene Tunney, Max Schmeling, Jack Sharkey, and Primo Carnera were at or near the top and Tony looked forward to the day when he would be in the ring with one of them. For now Tony focused on his training and preparation for the next opponent.

Tony's favorite meal had now become breakfast: sausage, three eggs looking at you, hash browns, milk, orange juice and whole wheat toast. "Mel, you gonna eat the rest of your hash browns?" Tony asked.

"No, holy cow Tony do you ever fill up. Christ you must have been a chow hound at home. No wonder your ma had to go out to work." Mel said.

"I get hungry," responded Tony as he scraped the rest of Mel's hash browns onto his plate.

A fight promoter from Philadelphia stepped into the restaurant and walked directly toward Tony and Mel.

"Man I'm glad I found you guys. I'm Sterling Morris and these are my associates."

"How can I help?" Mel asked.

"Do you mind if we sit down," Morris asked.

Mel reached out his hand and passed it to his right toward an empty chair and said, "Have a seat."

Morris moved his chair closer to the table and folded his arms and said, "I'm going to cut to the chase, Mel. We want to offer you and Tony a contract to fight two prospects I have back in Philly. We could have one fight here and if your boy gets lucky the next back east, maybe Philly."

Mel's eyes lit up while Tony focused on eating the rest of his and Mel's breakfast. "So Mr. Morris, I need to get Tony here to training, but follow us down the street and we can talk."

"Excellent," responded Morris, "let's go." Mel and Morris found a vacant office and shared small talk and then got down to business. Morris had a colleague who had two excellent prospects rising fast in Philly, but didn't want to pit them against each other. Big Tony from Detroit had become somewhat of an icon just because of his fight name. Just the thought of a Detroit fighter against a Philly fighter was enough of a money making draw.

Mel looked the contract over carefully. It contained a bonus with a win, he knew the promoter had a good reputation for being legitimate and fair, which was unusual. "Mr. Morris I like what I see, except for a few minor changes, but I need to send this to Tony's brother Vito Cosenza for his review."

"Is he one of those Chicago Mob guys," asked Morris.

"Mr. Morris, Vito has been looking out for his brother for 10 years and all I know is he is a successful businessman."

"Okay, if we can get this done in two weeks we'll have time to get this promoted with a major local venue," Morris said.

Within a week Vito had a copy of the contract. Vito provided a few changes and overall liked the opportunity it presented for his brother. He signed the contract and mailed it back to Mel. Three weeks later a fight was set as part of an undercard for a major title fight. Tony and Mel were both excited. There would be familiar faces including the cut man in Tony's corner. Mel researched Tony's opponent and called friends in the Philadelphia area to get insight into the rising star. The opponent was Jack Nelson, who was 8 and 0 with six knock outs. Tony saw his opportunity with Mel's pushing, he trained like never before. He had to: it was a step up to go to a six-round fight from his previous four-rounds. The big fight night was scheduled for July 4, 1934.

The crowd noise was deafening and the smoke-filled auditorium was not only asphyxiating to the non-smokers, it gave the appearance of being in the fog. Big Tony from Detroit and his entourage entered first. The size of the audience and the noise was overwhelming to Tony. As he stepped up onto the edge of the ring he paused and looked around. He had never seen this many people inside a hall this big. "Tony, keep moving," shouted Mel, as he pushed him through the ropes. "Tony, forget the crowd, focus on our training, what this guy can do and his weaknesses," Mel said. Next came Tony's opponent with far less fanfare, which was no surprise since Tony represented the pride of Detroit. Jack Nelson, a colored man, appeared to be on the paunchy side at 6' 2" he weighed in at 248 pounds, heavier than Big Tony, but with less reach. Big Tony's reception at his introduction was resounding while that for Nelson was followed with boos. The two tapped gloves and went to their respective corners.

The bell for round one rang and the two opponents went into battle. Jabs, jabs and more jabs were led by Tony while Jack hit back with defensive punches. The first round had action, but was a feeling-out round for both fighters. Round two featured more aggression by both fighters, and Big Tony clearly won. Round three was a draw as was round four.

At the end of round four Mel announced to Tony that Vito was in the audience with friends, and told him to show his stuff. "Tony, this fight is too close to call. I want you to follow up with combinations. Every time Nelson throws a left jab come with an overhand right and a left jab, boom, boom, like that," Mel touted. Big Tony only nodded.

Round five started with the bell and the fighters met. Both were tiring, but Big Tony had more in the tank. Nelson led with jabs and Tony blocked them. He thought of his brother and he wanted him to be proud. Just then Nelson came with a low jab, a perfect opportunity. Big Tony followed with an overhand right to Nelson's head and a left jab and a powerful overhand right. Nelson fell to the floor and could not make the final count. It was over and the crowd was going nuts. Big Tony from Detroit had overcome the boy from Philly. Tony raised his hands in joy and then checked on Nelson's wellbeing. Nelson was a worthy opponent and gave it his all.

Tony sat in his dressing room with Mel cutting the tape from his hands and the cut man tending to a minor cut at Tony's eye. Sweat was pouring from Tony's body and he was still catching his breath when the dressing room door opened. It was Vito with two body guards. "So Big Tony from Detroit, wow, you were something--like a Jack Dempsey," said Vito as he hugged his brother. Vito looked at the bruised and cut Tony and for the first time he was seriously concerned about Tony continuing in the sport, but said nothing.

"Vito," said an exhausted Tony, "the crowd loves me here in Detroit and I love them. I feel a connection. I don't want to ever let them down."

Vito gave Tony another hug and as tears came to his eyes he whispered in Tony's ear, "I love you. Pa would be proud."

Tony whispered back, "I love you too Vito." The brothers had a bond that could never be broken. They had lost their pa together, they grew up caring for each other, survived Tony's abduction, and survived and returned from the St. Paul Ice House adventure.

"Mel, you take care of this lug. I'm going back to my seat. I'll be in touch," Vito said.

Mel was looking at Tony's eye and he turned and said, "You bet I will."

CHAPTER 19

Clark Street

"Mean Mike we need to have that conversation I spoke of," Vito said.

"*Si* Vito, when and where?" asked Mean Mike.

"How about coming over to Nanu's for supper."

"I'd love to get a home cooked Italian dinner."

"Besides, Rose's boyfriend is visiting the family for the first time and this should be interesting--he's Irish," added Vito.

"Irish!" said Mean Mike with a sheepish laugh. "Where did she meet an Irish kid?"

"She said she met him at Holy Sacrament," answered Vito.

"How does Antonio feel about Rose being with an Irish kid?" asked Mean Mike.

"Well I assume he is Catholic so he may be okay with it," Vito said. The meal for the night was a surprise it was corned beef and cabbage and was not bad. Everyone got a chance to meet Rose's boyfriend. He was a good looking young man, about 6 foot 1 inch tall, pale looking compared to the Mediterranean's, still had a few childhood freckles, and reddish-blond hair.

Rose's boyfriend appeared intimidated until he said, "Now don't take this the wrong way, but go very easy on the *vino* because you'll get a gut ache like never before if you don't. *Vino* doesn't mix well with cabbage!"

His comment broke the ice with laughter because he was right. After the meal Vito asked to be excused with Mike.

The two walked to the grape arbor with a glass of *vino* and sat. "Mike," Vito started, "you see my pa's car?"

"Yes, it's been there forever and I don't know why?" Mean Mike said.

"Mike, my pa's car was tampered with. His accident was planned out--he was murdered," explained Vito.

"Damn, that's serious business Vito," responded Mean Mike, "very serious."

Vito nodded, "I think my pa was involved with either the North or South Side Gang. I need you to ask some of the older guys about Pa's activity. Someone has to know something."

"Mike, I know this is something that you may not want to get involved in and you can drop out anytime."

"I'll do that Vito, but I'll have to be very careful. If I talk to more than one it will create suspicion and could cause trouble if there was any involvement. But we need to talk to one of the South Side guys or someone associated with them like Carmine The Weasel Francisco. He always knows more than he should--let's start with Carmine. I loved your pa, he was good to me. I know he could have been an up-and-comer with the Capone Mob, but I think he liked to be on his own and wasn't interested in bootlegging. I never said anything because at that time it was of no consequence and I was young myself and just started as a Soldier. I'm warning you, old rumors labeled Angelo a safe cracker."

"I understand there will be some disappointments. I need to see where the alleged accident occurred first," added Vito.

"I can take you there tomorrow," responded Mean Mike.

Vito had already moved to the north side of Waukegan so he would be close to the Alvano Family business and not that far from Gwen who was always on his mind. He and Mean Mike drove Vito's car to the north side of Chicago and the Clark Street accident site. The accident happened within a few blocks of the St. Valentine's Day Massacre which was in the Moran-controlled area of town. What would an Italian be doing alone in a neighborhood controlled by Irish? The street had a slight downhill slope. He had to be going fast for the damage that was done and to lose control and crash in the river. "Mike, take my car and come back in 25 minutes," Vito asked. "I'm going to snoop around a little bit."

"Be careful," Mean Mike said.

Vito knocked at the door of the nearest row home. A young woman answered the door and said she had only lived there three years, but an older couple across the street had lived in the neighborhood since before the war. Vito hurried across the street to the row home, which had a door mat that read, "Welcome to the Curry's." Vito knocked on the door and an older woman answered and said, "Hello." Vito introduced himself and explained that he needed information from several years back. The woman said, "I'm Kay and my husband is Earl. Maybe I can help." Earl sat quietly and Vito could sense he was perhaps senile. "Would you like to sit down?" asked Kay. Vito obliged and asked if she remembered anything about the accident that had happened nearly 13 years earlier. Kay answered, "Yes, it happened at night and it took a long time for the police or an ambulance to arrive." She added, "a lot of people heard the noise from the accident, but I don't recall if anyone saw it happen."

At night, Vito thought, he didn't know it happened at night and why were the police so slow? "Mrs. Curry, had you ever seen that car or my pa before?"

"Why yes. I may seem a little nosey, but he was here several times visiting, I think Max Murphy." She paused for a moment. "Your pa would visit with a big guy."

"Thank you so much Mrs. Curry. Do you mind if I come back?"

"No I don't and maybe I'll have coffee next time."

Mean Mike was just driving by and Vito hopped in. "Vito, don't tell me a thing unless I really need to know," requested Mean Mike. Vito motioned yes with a nod.

Carmine Francisco was working as a stock boy in an Italian grocery store located near the north side of Chicago. Alvano had arranged for Carmine to work at an honest job. Mean Mike and Vito approached him at work and as soon as Carmine saw Mean Mike he became nervous once again. Mean Mike greeted him, "Hello Carmine."

"Oh shit now what have I done? I'm doing a good job and I thank the Don," responded Carmine.

"No, relax, we want to see if you can help again."

"What can I do to help?" Carmine said. Mean Mike said he needed some information on Vito Cosenza's pa's death. Carmine said, "Now you know I don't hang with the same crowd anymore. I remember Angelo. I didn't know him well, but I do remember he was smart and really nobody knew him that well. You know asking questions could get me into trouble."

"That was clear from the beginning, but if you learn something you must keep it until we contact you again in a few weeks and I will sweeten your pocket," responded Vito.

"We can do business. I may be an old fart, but I can get information in very clever ways."

"Good, we'll see you in three weeks," Vito said.

CHAPTER 20

Business for the Family

With the Revenue Act of 1932 and the gas taxes in Wisconsin, Illinois and Indiana, the money Vito was bringing into the Alvano Family escalated. It rivaled the sale of beer and alcohol, which in the past had to be shared with the South Side Gang. Federal and state revenue acts were helping him make money for the Family. Vito also started supplying tobacco products and vending machines to service stations and grocery stores and kept the taxes. He had little problem purchasing petroleum or tobacco products wholesale and the number of employees expanded. He developed a plan to add pinball machines and games of chance.

The businesses organized by Vito depended solely on the incompetence of state and federal internal revenue agencies. The bogus companies that had been set up took an enormous amount of time and detail to maintain as clandestine. Post office boxes and rural postal addresses had to be maintained to avoid suspicion, which was accomplished by trusted soldiers who used disguises. When a letter from a revenue service was received, an apologetic response was made after a short time. After the second letter the bogus company was dissolved and a new one was made to replace it. Petroleum delivery trucks marked in the past were now seldom marked. They were always on time to keep the proprietor's happy.

The more Vito learned the more he expanded the Family business. They went further into Wisconsin and to the fringe of Iowa and deeper into

Indiana following populated areas. Most venders were accommodating, but from time to time a heavy hand would have to be used.

Vito thought, with his recent successes for the Family business, what better time to talk to the Don about his search for his pa's killer. The following afternoon after a sit down Family meeting, Vito asked Don Alvano if he could speak to him in private, something that seldom happened, but his request was granted. After the two were alone in the Don's office a few moments of silence passed. Alvano lit a cigar just as Vito initiated the conversation. "Don Alvano, the loss of my pa has weighed heavy on my heart and I have reason to believe his death was premeditated and that his car was tampered with."

"I understand. I lost my Father to the Black Hand when I was 12 years old and his loss has troubled me too," explained Alvano. "Now what is it you need from me?"

"In three weeks I need to search out a man but I don't know where yet. I'll need some time to put all of this together," requested Vito.

"*Si,*" responded Alvano. "Don't involve the Family or compromise our standing with any of the Families to the east and keep me appraised."

Vito kissed the back of the Don's hand, "Yes of course. Thank you for your trust and I'll contact Mean Mike with anything I learn." Vito was set. He knew exactly what he would do from here.

CHAPTER 21

Philadelphia Fight Night

It was well known to the boxing world that Philadelphia produced some of the greatest boxers in the world. Philadelphia would also be another opportunity for Big Tony from Detroit to rise in the rankings and become a contender. Since his fight with Nelson, Tony had two more fights locally in the following six months and was now 9 and 0. Morris sent a second contract to Mel, but this time the fight would be an undercard in Philadelphia. Mel followed the same procedure of reviewing it himself and sending a copy to Vito.

The boxing crowd was opening up to Big Tony and Mel. Mel and his fighter were becoming well known because Big Tony was developing into a prospect. Sport writers were hounding the two at every opportunity because now Big Tony had a chance, with a few more wins, to challenge the champ.

Jack the Shark Menzel slapped his hands together with delight when he found out his next opponent, Big Tony from Detroit, had only 9 fights. Menzel was called the Shark because he tried to cut his opponents around the eyes by rubbing the tape and tie strings of his gloves across their face. Menzel was 21 – 0 and 1, with a very controversial draw. Some fight fans thought there was big money behind Menzel and that the fight was fixed. Had it not been for the fact that the fight with Big Tony was promoted by Morris there might have been a lot of suspicion, but Morris was squeaky clean. However, "Nicko" Teboundini, an underboss in a dominant Philadelphia Family, was a fight fan and had been winning big-time bets with Menzel as his boy.

Mel pushed Big Tony as hard as he could; he was never easy to train for. After completing his last workout a day before the weigh-in ceremony, a crowd of local reporters focused on Big Tony and Mel. "So you think you can take the Shark," said a small statured reporter. Before Big Tony could answer he was hit with two more questions.

"Guys," Big Tony shouted, "take your time. I can only answer one question at a time."

"So answer the first question--can you take the Shark," yelled another writer.

"Well, I've trained hard and deserve a chance to fight Mr. Menzel and I will give it my best. After all it's not like he is invincible. There was some controversy to his draw." The questions continued with some directed at stimulating bad blood between the two fight camps.

After the interviews Big Tony commented to Mel, "Man, were some of those questions stupid or just dumb?"

"They were pretty typical Tony. Most of these guys don't have much and just try to make stuff up to sell papers," Mel answered.

On fight night Big Tony was as ready as he would ever be now it was an eight-round fight. The venue was fantastic, but Big Tony was not overwhelmed. His fights in Detroit had prepared him for big ones like this and he was set to seize the opportunity. He knew Vito couldn't be there nor his pa, but they were both in his heart and he would make them proud. This time the roar of the crowd was for the Shark, who entered the ring after Big Tony. Menzel already had bad hearing, but now it would be worse.

With the formalities of the introductions and the instructions by the ref at center ring over, the two gladiators met after the bell to do battle. Tony started with continuous left jabs while the Shark tried to end it quick with wild right hooks. By the third round the Shark changed his tactic and switched to south paw which confused Big Tony. The Shark caught him with a left hook that dropped him. Tony came off the floor at the eight count and was dazed. The Shark moved in for the kill and threw one quick jab as the bell rung. "Don't say a thing," yelled Mel as Big Tony stumbled to his chair. "Shake it off, he got lucky," yelled Mel.

"Holy shit Mel, I'm not deaf," said Big Tony as he finally caught his wits. The bell rang and Big Tony was back into it throwing combinations like he never had before. The Shark was caught off guard. He expected a devastated Big Tony, but instead caught an upper cut followed by a crushing overhand right that put the Shark down for the first time and ended the fight. Big Tony went wild with joy of the victory and leaped like a kangaroo, then waved to the few fans he had.

Nicko was furious; he just lost five Gs on his favorite boy. He was a vengeful Mobster and would take it out on one of the fighters. This would be the last fight for the Shark because three weeks later Nicko would have three of his thugs bust the Shark's hands.

The locker room for Big Tony had no room to spare. Big Tony had just given Philly's best rising star a lights-out demonstration. Some of the sportswriters told Big Tony he was lucky while others acknowledged his boxing skills as exceptional. Through all the chatter one voice stood out: "Big Tony, Big Tony it's me Anthony Falduto, I'm your cousin from New York."

"My cousin? I don't recall hearing of you," Big Tony said.

Falduto worked his way closer and shook Big Tony's hand vigorously. "I'm actually your second cousin through your grandfather's sister," Falduto said. "Let me take you guys to dinner after you clean up."

"I have to have the Doc check me out and clean up first and then Mel and I go to breakfast," Big Tony said.

"Then breakfast it is," answered Falduto. Falduto provided Big Tony with some family history and explained that he followed the fights and saw a familiar name, Pontillo. Falduto was interested in the Pontillo family and how they were doing. He had made the trip to Philly just to see his cousin fight.

CHAPTER 22

Vito's Investigation

Vito was clever at concealing his investigation of his pa's death, keeping the Don posted and maintaining a high profile with the Alvano Family leadership. He continued to provide money-making schemes that fed off the needs of the public and the incompetence of federal and state revenue agencies. He had two short term objectives: first, find out who Murphy was, and find him Second, find out who the big guy was who would accompanied his pa to Murphy's row home. It was time to consult Carmine and to see if Mean Mike had learned anything. The sooner he got Mean Mike out of the picture the safer it would be for him. In time he would bring Big Tony into the quest, but not until he had more conclusive information.

Carmine The Weasel was not hard to find. If he wasn't working in a grocery store he would be in his apartment or a small bar near the Carlton. Vito would try the grocery store first. Vito entered Tanuto's Italian Market and grabbed a grocery basket. He slowly worked his way through the produce section, then the beer and wine section, before he saw Carmine in the Deli. He was not shaken this time when Vito greeted him, but instead he smiled and whispered he had some information. "It's mostly old rumors, but it still may be of help," explained Carmine. "Can you meet me at my apartment Saturday at one in the afternoon? I'll write the address for you."

"Sure," said Vito as he took the note from Carmine. Vito continued shopping: Tanuto's had always been a great place to shop for products straight from Italy.

Vito's drive to determine who was behind his pa's death was almost all consuming. He had to force himself to pay attention to his business dealings for the Alvano Family, maintain communication, and to make sure Gwen knew she was important. However, he had almost lost track of Tony. Damn, he thought, he had a big fight in Philadelphia and I forgot about it. Vito planned to check up on Tony after one more visit with Carmine.

Vito disguised himself as a street bum with his complement of worn clothes and a brown bag with Kentucky rye. Vito parked his car a block from Carmine's and walked the distance, posing as a bum so as not to raise any suspicion. Vito was armed with a new Colt .45 automatic he kept under his jacket. Carmine opened his door cautiously after Vito knocked.

"It's me Vito, let me in."

"Holy shit, I thought you were a street bum looking for a handout," Carmine said. "Have a seat." Carmine cleared away old newspapers and magazines and then offered Vito a beer.

"Do you have any *vino*?" asked Vito.

"Ya, if it doesn't taste like vinegar," Carmine said. He poured Vito a glass of *vino* and cleared a spot for him to sit. "I didn't have much to go on, but I did learn a bit that may surprise you."

"Go on, I need to know everything straight up," Vito said.

Carmine went on to say that Vito's pa was on the fringe of the South Side Gang and had committed an armed robbery or two, but not in Chicagoland. "Your pa was apparently a small-time crook who may have made it big-time in the end. I also learned he became a very good safe cracker."

"I was worried I'd hear that, but I loved him and he loved us and I need to learn more. Can you find out who Max Murphy is? He lived on Clark Street over 10 years ago."

"I'll do my best," Carmine said. He would have to be careful not to draw any attention to his inquisitiveness. Vito handed Carmine the unopened bottle of Kentucky rye and $20. Next he would consult Mean Mike.

All Vito could think about on the drive back to Waukegan was what he suspected all along: that his pa was an outlaw. He just didn't know how much trouble his pa was in, but his death was likely linked to an act of crime. Vito met with Mean Mike and only learned that his pa was outside of the Alvano Family and not well known to the Chicagoland underworld. It did not answer the question of whether or not he was known further east. So he would focus on facts from 12 years ago that occurred in other known Mob areas like Detroit, Cleveland, St. Louis, Memphis, or Toledo. The biggest news from Mean Mike was that his pa hung out with Bruno Salvatore. Was this the big guy Mrs. Curry spoke of? He had enough information from Mean Mike and wouldn't ask him to research anymore. My God, he thought, I may die trying to figure any more out. A vendetta was due if he did discover who killed his pa.

CHAPTER 23

Big Tony Sees the Dark Side of Boxing

"Tony, I think we need to expand our team," Mel said. "I'm over my head out here. If we want to get better fights and a chance at a championship fight we need a manager who understands the business better than I do."

Tony turned from the radio he was listening to and said, "Mel, I thought we were doing good."

"I want to head things off before I get you and my sorry ass in too deep with these contracts. You see, we will be seeing must-win clauses and more," Mel said. "For example, the fights are arranged so far out you might need a fight here or there to keep sharp. So if you get beat by a chump it makes you a chump. A top scale fighter won't waste his time on you because you wouldn't offer a good pay day." Then Mel shouted, "And come back away from that radio--it will ruin your hearing and I can't compete with it."

Tony complied. Mel had become his guardian. After all, he had promised Vito he would look after Tony. "What's next in our search for an honest manager? I know there are a few who wouldn't be there for us," Tony said.

"We are in a low time in boxing and it may be a tough thing to do, but I'll do my best to find someone," Mel said. "Remember those films we watched of the training of some of the fighters that Two Ton Tony Galenta fought?"

"Ya, I remember. You said to watch the other fighters and they looked good and still lost."

"Exactly, that's because Galenta had the Mob behind him and fights were fixed with either payoffs to judges or the opponents were bought off," Mel said. "Galenta likely didn't even know what was going on. After breakfast tomorrow morning I'll see what I can find out from Morris."

That morning Mel and Tony had a quick visit with Morris. To Mel's surprise, Morris was reluctant to recommend anyone and said he would put the word out that Mel was looking for a manager. Morris also said that he had been contacted by the manager of a contender who was hoping to schedule a fight with Primo Carnera. "How soon would that be?" asked Mel.

"I'll have them contact you and you two can get back to me because we could use an undercard in six weeks," Morris said. "Can you manage Big Tony for one more fight?"

"I can do that." Mel and Tony stepped out of Morris's office and walked the few blocks to their motel, past the typical strip lounges that proliferated the older less affluent parts of Philadelphia, and then past a series of row homes. That night Tony would make a new friend. Her name was Peaches.

It was after 3 a.m. when Tony rolled into his hotel room. "Where the hell have you been Tony?" Mel yelled.

"I've been visiting with a new girlfriend, Peaches," answered Tony. "I think I'm in love again."

"Oh crap, Tony. We need to keep you in training, not chasing a new girlfriend," answered Mel.

"Oh Mel, she won't be a problem."

The next afternoon there was a knock at the hotel room door. Mel opened the door and two well-dressed goons were standing there. Only one spoke. "Mr. Thompson we would like you to come with us. Tony can stay, and don't worry we are here to take you to our boss for a business deal." Mel reluctantly complied, since he knew they were already in over their heads and from here it was a matter of survival.

115

Mel was escorted to a black Cadillac and within 20 minutes the door was opened for him and he was led into the back room of the Midnight Lounge. "Good afternoon Mr. Thompson," came an unfamiliar voice. "I'm your boy's new manager, and we will still employ you as his trainer."

Mel quickly responded, "Wait just a minute. Who says you're his new manager?"

"I'm sorry Mr. Thompson, my name is Vincent Walthurs. You can call me Vince and I'll call you Mel. We have a contract for you to sign. Don't worry, I'll give you a few moments to review it," Walthurs said. "You have no other options because no one else will pick your boy up—or you for that matter." Mel was right: they had no sooner won a fight in Philly and already they were sucked into the Mob. For now, he would sign and follow instructions. He thought for a moment how Vito would react without knowing what he was committing to and said, "Vince you need to know Tony's brother is Vito Cosenza and has been involved in all Tony's contracts."

"I know," said Walthurs, "you leave Vito to me. I guarantee he'll be okay with this." Within two hours Mel was returned to his motel room and greeted Tony.

"Tony, I have good news and bad news. What do you want to hear first?" he asked.

"How about the good news," Tony said.

"We have three fights in the next 19 months, and we make good money with wins. The bad news is our manager is Vincent Walthurs and I think he has Mob connections," Mel said.

"We just went from bad to worse—you just can't get away from these guys. For now we just play along and fight until we find a way out. To run now could cost us our lives, so we just have to survive. Walthurs said he would take care of Vito, I don't know what he meant."

"Vito can take care of himself. Have a warm Blatz. I brought it from Kenosha. We'll work through this," Tony said. "By the way I have a date with Peaches again. She doesn't get off till 1 a.m. so I'll be a little late."

Walthurs provided a decent training facility, the expenses were reasonable and he did involve Vito. Mel and Big Tony were up to the challenge in Philly to fight top-notch prospects, but something was wrong.

During the fourth round of Big Tony's third fight he told Mel, "What do you bet if I hit this guy with a good left hook he flops?"

"Let's see it," whispered Mel. Just as predicted, Big Tony from Detroit dropped his third so-called up and coming fighter within 20 seconds of the bell of the fourth round. Big Tony from Detroit was now 13 and 0.

"Mel, I haven't pissed blood since my fight with Menzel, not that I want to, but these so—called prospects that Walthurs is booking for us are hyped-up chumps. Not one of them has hit me hard enough to notice and none have gone much more than three rounds."

Mel quickly responded, "Something is up, and I think I know what is going to happen within the next year. Did you notice how your publicity has taken off like never before, but the odds on you are always low, you're the underdog. Someone is controlling some strings with all this." Mel scratched the side of his head as if thinking and said, "I'll bet you get a title fight soon and the odds will change again."

Big Tony was working on a speed bag with a half a dozen sports writers watching. Tony was doing some of his rhythm work on the heavy bag: left, left, left, crossover right, left, left, left, and crossover right. One of the writers shouted, "I heard you have a title fight coming up. Pretty good opportunity for such a young guy."

Tony stopped and looked at the informant and asked, "Where did you hear that?"

"Oh, it's a rumor that started floating around last week."

Mel stepped in, "Let's go Tony, time to spar." After a half an hour of sparring Walthurs walked into the gym with his goons.

"Mel," Walthurs shouted, "I have some news, but let's find an office."

As Mel followed Walthurs to a vacant office he popped three sticks of Juicy Fruit gum in his mouth, something he did when he got nervous. "So what's up," asked Mel.

"Our boy has a tune-up for a possible championship fight." Walthurs put a thumb up and smiled, "Tony has to be ready in three weeks, and the fight is at Madison Square Garden as an undercard to Carnera and Shepard. The winner gets to fight the heavy weight champ of the world. We got class A training facilities near Lake Placid so everything will be fine with the New York State Boxing Commission." Within two days Big Tony and Mel were on their way to Lake Placid. Big Tony was scheduled to fight the second-ranked boxer from Europe, an Englishman by the name of Eric Danbury who was relatively unknown in the states.

Walthurs thought he had everything set. Big Tony and Mel would be like all the others and he and a few of his buddies would have a big payday. First was the publicity exhorting Big Tony's skills. He would set up an entourage of sports writers, and Big Tony's sparing partners would be subpar, making him look good. Walthurs would have one of his goons put false rumors out on the street that Danbury had a glass jaw and had lost his last two fights by knock out. The odds makers would have Big Tony heavily favored and Walthurs would ensure he flopped and Danbury would win, making a big payday.

Mel prepared Big Tony as hard as ever for a shot at the championship. But, it was easy to get complacent: the scenery was gorgeous, the girls followed Big Tony like the Pied Piper and everyone in town was pleasant. Big Tony and Mel still felt something was up. "Mel," asked Tony, "where in the hell are these sparing partners coming from? They all look good on paper, but when we spar they don't have the quickness or the attitude of the guys in Philly or Detroit."

"I noticed that too. I think something is up," Mel said.

"Too tight?" asked Mel, as he taped Tony's gloves on for another hour of sparring.

"No, not at all. Wipe the sweat from my forehead would you? Man it's a hot one today," said Tony.

"It sure is," Mel said as he wiped Tony's forehead. "I still don't know for sure what Walthurs is up to. We have four days until the fight and Walthurs is due in tomorrow."

"Don't you think tomorrow will be the day we learn what's up?" Tony asked.

"You're right, tomorrow will be the day, we need to have a plan and we'll talk about that tonight," whispered Mel. That night the two decided that under no circumstances would they throw the fight. If Walthurs or anyone else approached them they would be casual about it, and would also make arrangements to skip out after the fight. For that Tony would see if his second cousin Faldutoo could help because they had never been near the "Garden".

"Tony, go clean up and I'll treat for supper tonight," Mel said.

Tony turned slowly to look at Mel. They were the last ones in the gym. "You'll treat? What's the occasion?"

"The occasion is, this will be our last supper in this life because if you win I think we'll be done for and I'm scared," Mel said. "Tony, what's more important: our lives or our integrity?"

"You know the answer to that Mel."

"Well, you never know. Maybe we're making it a bigger deal than it is."

An hour later the two were in Profetto's Italian restaurant ordering their favorite, spaghetti. Ten minutes later Walthurs came in with his two goons and walked directly to their table. "I thought I would find you two here," he said. Walthurs casually looked around the neighboring tables to ensure everyone was engaged in their own business then looked at Tony and Mel and proceeded with, "Boys I'm going to explain some things to you once and I expect you will comply, an arrangement has been made and it's simple. Tony in the fifth round you'll take a left hook from Danbury and you'll hit the floor for the ten count. Don't worry, I promise you we'll make up for it in the future because if you behave you'll get your title fight."

Tony looked at Walthurs held up a meat ball on his fork and said, "These are pretty good meat balls but I like my ma's a whole lot better."

"You gotta be shiting me are you listening to me," whispered an angry Walthurs.

"Sure he is," whispered Mel. "We expected this and it's no big deal."

Walthurs looked toward Tony and then to Mel and said, "Good you understand." The waiter returned to take Walthurs' order.

"Wait," said Mel, "do you think we're saps? We want to know what our pay is now and to get paid before the fight."

Walthurs frowned briefly and then smiled, "Are you kidding it doesn't work that way." Walthurs got up and left the restaurant.

Back at the motel Mel had second thoughts on Tony going all out and trying to win and not throw the fight. Mel called out, "Tony, I think we need to think this through. We're dead chumps if we win this fight. Walthurs will put his goons on us and kill us for sure, and nobody will find our bodies." Tony immediately became argumentative.

"What the hell are you saying? We lose the fight? Bull crap, I don't let myself down and I don't let my fans down."

"No, no, no we can't win. It will all be okay. I know it," argued Mel. "We got to lose."

"I'm not throwing the fight, Mel," Tony shouted. He thought, I need to talk to Vito. Tony was upset that when push came to shove, Mel had given the appearance of a spineless coward, and Tony could never trust his judgment in the future. Tony felt betrayed. He was done with Mel regardless of the final outcome. The two argued for ten more minutes before Tony decided to appease Mel by saying, "Okay Mel, I'll go down this time." Tony saw a different Mel: he was scared stiff for his life.

"Good," said Mel, "then we're done arguing. I'll still arrange for someone to pick us up after the fight."

After Tony and Mel had gone to bed, Tony waited to hear Mel's snoring before he slipped out of the room. Tony went directly to the most secluded pay phone in the motel and called Vito. "Vito, it's Tony."

"Tony—good to hear from my favorite successful brother," answered Vito.

"Vito, I got trouble. Our new manager wants me to throw my big fight and Mel has sided with him. I don't want to, and I can't trust Mel, he's a coward," Tony said. Tony explained in detail what had happened: the publicity, the bookies, the odds in his favor to win, and the promise of a championship fight.

"I think I know what's going on," responded Vito. "We have a few days, so call me back tomorrow about noon my time and I'll have a plan." Vito immediately started making calls to bookie friends and to Kaiser. The next morning he consulted with Alvano and some of his associates. Another plan was formulated that could help Tony and make a payday.

At noon Central Time, Tony called Vito. "What am I to do?" Tony asked.

"Tony, I talked to our bookies and Alvano after our discussion last night. Are you convinced you can beat this chump for sure?"

Without hesitation Tony said, "Yes."

Vito said, "So here's the plan: the last afternoon before the fight, fake a right shoulder injury. Our bookies will ensure there is an odds swing toward the chump at the last minute. I mean, we have big money on you." Vito continued, "Your manager likely has big bucks on the chump Danbury as well as some other thugs. With the odds swing they may be confused and not change bets. Now, at the end of the fight I'll be there in your dressing room with a couple guys and get you out, but we leave Mel."

"We have a cousin in New York, Anthony Falduto, he will help. I met him after a recent fight and talked to him once since then," Tony said. "He knows the Madison Square Garden borough well."

"Give me his number and I'll call Falduto." Vito wanted to be sure Tony understood the plan and said. "Tony do you understand? We leave Mel."

"Mel said he would have a buddy drive us off."

"Forget Mel. He is out of this picture. I'll have my two body guards Phil and Dominick help too. You go with me, do you understand?" Vito said.

"I got it Vito and I promise I will win this fight. Either way, my career as a boxer is over."

At the weigh-in just before the fight dozens of reporters and a few bookies stood by. "Big Tony, I heard Danbury lost his last two fights. What do you think?" shouted a reporter.

"I think I need to weigh-in boys, no speculation from me. I'm here to fight and win," answered Big Tony.

Tony turned quickly and grabbed his shoulder as if in pain. "Say, what's wrong Tony? What are you hiding with the shoulder?" asked a reporter.

"Nothing," shouted Tony, "I'm fine."

Loud whispers went up throughout the crowd of reporters and bookies. One bookie said, "Something is up," and the others agreed.

Danbury stood by and said nothing. He scowled at Tony as the two faced off. Tony couldn't help himself and said, "I've seen meat balls that look better than you so maybe that's what I'll call you."

Danbury was enraged at the insult and responded, "When I finish with you you'll look like a meat ball after a healthy shit." Tony burst into laughter and saw the opportunity to feign an injured shoulder again.

Vito called Falduto and he agreed to help. Vito would bring bodyguards and Falduto knew the borough around Madison Square Garden and could prove to be a big help.

"Walthurs, every buck I got is on Danbury. Your boy better take the fall in this fight," said a grouchy Nicko. "What is it I hear he has a bum shoulder?"

"Ya that's what I saw at the weigh-in. All that does is increase our chances of winning. Besides he's still taking the dive," answered Walthurs. "I have all my coins on Danbury too. So if he doesn't dive he and Mel die and they know it."

Nicko said, "You're a stiff too if I lose again because of your screwing up." The two were so convinced Tony would hit the floor they didn't even pay attention to the odds which were shifting rapidly in favor of Danbury.

"You took four sticks of Juicy Fruit Mel, what are you nervous about?" asked Tony.

"This is a big night in a lot of ways," answered Mel. "We don't know what's going to face us after the fight, it could be very dangerous. So I went ahead made arrangements for an old Army buddy to pick up our stuff at the hotel room and meet us behind the Garden as soon as the fight is over."

The conversation was interrupted when the dressing room door opened. "Ten minutes to introductions, boys," a voice shouted.

Mel and Big Tony were joined by the cut man and a corner assistant to Mel. "Looks like you're ready," said the cut man to Tony.

"As ready as I will ever be," Tony said. "I'm not gonna let my fans in Detroit down." He winked to Mel. Mel smiled, convinced Tony would take the fall.

The four men watched the locker room clock. "Let's go, it's time," Mel shouted.

Big Tony had the second fight of the night as an undercard. The previous fight was a brawl with both fighters bleeding like hogs in a slaughterhouse. It took Garden staff a few extra minutes to clean the mat. The customary entrance of the two fighters took place with Mel delaying Big Tony's entrance to increase suspense. Danbury had already entered and was getting bored with the wait as the crowd began to chant "Big Tony, Big Tony, Big Tony." It was an exhilarating feeling for Big Tony and his entourage because he wasn't sure what his ovation would be like.

Big Tony and his corner men entered at cheering that shook Madison Square Gardens. Many in attendance were waving small Italian flags. "I think you got all of Little Italy here tonight guys," Mel shouted under a deafening cheer. Mel was partly right—many in attendance were Italian or Sicilian. Walthurs wasn't Italian. The two fighters met at the center of the ring and touched gloves after the referee's instructions. It was obvious both were ready to do battle. Tony couldn't help himself with the meat and shit story and started to laugh again. There wasn't a feeling out in the first round because both fighters exchanged heavy hits like they had never experienced before. Danbury was burned because of the booing that he received before the fight, Big Tony's cheering support and Big Tony's laughing. Big Tony was excited because of all the cheering. The two fighters pummeled each other for the next four rounds and were both thankful it was only going to be an eight-round fight. In the fifth round Walthurs, sitting in a front row seat, was visibly anxious, smoking cigarettes faster than he could get them to his lips, and at the end of the fifth round was visibly upset. Danbury, who was known for a terrific left hook, had caught Big Tony twice in the fifth and all he did was win the round.

"Tony, I can tell Walthurs is pissed," whispered Mel to his panting boxer. Big Tony only managed to smile behind a cut lip. Mel gave Big Tony fight instructions as the whole corner hoped the sixth round would be the last with a win but for Mel. Mel wanted a loss since Tony was supposed to fall in the fifth. In the sixth, each fighter took jabs at each other and exchanged body shots.

Late in the sixth round Danbury caught Tony with an upper-cut that leveled him and Danbury started to celebrate. It was only the second time Tony had kissed the floor in his short career; for a moment, he thought he was done. He could hear the ref counting: one, two three, four. Tony thought about Vito and his fans--this blow was not going to be his end. Tony was wobbled, but picked himself up off the floor as the bell rang. Mel slapped him a couple times and whispered, "Why did you get up?" Tony didn't respond. He was ready for round seven. Big Tony was hit immediately with a left hook and was waiting for another left hook from Danbury. When it finally came with a minute left in the seventh round he countered with a hard left jab followed with an overhand right that delivered the blow to end the fight. Big Tony wasn't reserved this time. He was elated and jumped from corner to corner waving to fans as his cut man chased him.

Mel had ducked out. He looked to Walthurs seat as he left the ring and it was empty. Nicko was so furious he could not speak and went looking for Walthurs.

Big Tony's dressing room was crowded with reporters all calling out questions. Mel shouted, "For crying out loud one at a time." A few moments later Walthurs could be seen in the crowd. He was more than just steamed.

He looked at Mel and said with his lips, "You bastard you're going to die."

Mel smiled and said, "I love you too." This made Walthurs all the madder, since he'd bet tens of thousands of dollars on Danbury to win. Just as Walthurs left the room Mel shouted to Big Tony, "We can visit more with these gentlemen after you clean up."

CHAPTER 24

Life Goes On

Big Tony showered quickly and dressed while Mel had his cut man arrange for a diversion. The cut man told the reporters to meet Big Tony and Mel in an adjacent room that was larger, after the championship fight which was a few minutes from beginning. The news media's priority was to interview the winner of that fight. Then the cut man retrieved a large laundry bin and rolled it into the dressing room. Mel and Big Tony then dressed themselves in janitorial staff uniforms and slipped out of the room pushing the laundry bin. When Tony saw Vito and Falduto he casually walked toward him, leaving Mel. Vito looked toward Mel and told him that Tony would be leaving with him and that Mel was on his own. Mel didn't hesitate and left the cart. Vito told Tony to jump into the cart and he and Falduto covered him with linen. They pushed the cart down a hall way to a side door marked, Staff Only. They went in through the door and then to a second door that opened to an alley. There waiting was Dominick in a car. Falduto jumped in the driver side while Vito and Tony got in the back. Falduto drove them away from Madison Square Garden. Falduto guided them for several miles before they dropped him off at a lounge. The three drove west for several hours before they stopped at a motor inn in Essex, Maryland, just outside Baltimore where Phil was waiting. They stayed overnight with Vito's two bodyguards. The next morning Tony stayed with Phil while Vito and Dominick returned to New York to collect his substantial winnings. Walthurs was cleaned out as was the furious Nicko who was still looking for Walthurs, who was on the lamb.

After escaping out a side door Mel and the cut man went different directions. Mel met his old World War I Army buddy, Easy Plumber, who was waiting in his car. The two had survived several battles in France and had kindled a renewed friendship in recent months. Mel was unconcerned for Tony because he was with Vito. The two drove for an hour to a small motor inn in New Jersey. There they held up for several days. What they didn't know was that they were followed by two of Walthurs' goons.

Two days after Mel and his buddy entered the motor inn. Mel told Easy he could leave without him. It would be much safer. It didn't matter: his buddy would stay. "If you're going to do a fool thing and stay with me," then we need to leave tonight," Mel said. Easy casually walked out a side door with his suitcase into the dark, started the car and waited for Mel. Mel quickly grabbed his bag, walked out the same door and got in the car. Easy took off before Mel had a chance to close his passenger side door. The two goons were waiting. Mel and Easy were met with a flurry of bullets from two Thompson submachine guns. Mel and Easy were struck numerous times. Easy lost control of the car and it hit an embankment and rolled. The goons stopped and shot both three more times.

After a week in Waukegan, Vito and Tony found out that Mel and Easy had been murdered. A looming question was if Tony was implicated in their murder, and if he was a material witness. The authorities needed to understand he too was fleeing for his life. "Tony, I think we need to see if the cops are looking for you," Vito said. "You were with me and my boys all the time so you have an iron-clad alibi. Regardless, they don't have a thing on you."

"I'm sorry to hear Mel was killed. He was a good man, he just got scared," Tony said.

Vito added, "Before we contact the cops we get a lawyer and I know a good one. The timing of all of this may complicate what I have to tell you about Pa. Sit tight and let me have my man talk to the cops in New York. By the way I'm going to talk to Walthurs too. Before that I'll have to talk to the Don and make sure I have his okay to explain a few things to Walthurs."

Vito had a sit down with Alvano and Kaiser and explained how they escaped from the Garden, with Falduto's help, and that Walthurs likely had Mel and Easy murdered. Vito asked Alvano's permission to use the Family name to protect Tony from Walthurs. Alvano agreed saying he always liked Tony, and had respect for his courage. The next morning Vito, Phil, and Dominick were on their way to New York to visit Walthurs.

Walthurs had finally tired of running from Nicko and expected the two would have it out soon. What Walthurs did not expect was a visit from Vito. After arriving in New York Vito and his two body guards took a cab to Walthurs office. "Mr. Walthurs, there is a man here to see you by the name of Vito Cosenza," said the night club manager.

"Send him in," Walthurs said, as he reached into his desk for a snub nose .38. As Vito walked in with Phil and Dominick Walthurs said, "You must be Tony's brother!"

"Good guess Mr. Walthurs, and slowly take your hand out of your desk drawer. There is no need for violence. I'm a peaceful man." Walthurs slowly withdrew his hand.

"You know I lost my ass because of your brother and so did a few other chumps," Walthurs shouted.

"Calm down Mr. Walthurs. I think after I explain a few things you will go on with your life and Tony will go on with his," Vito said. "You expected my brother to take a dive which was your first mistake." Vito's conversation with Walthurs was abruptly interrupted when two goons burst in with guns drawn. Quickly Phil and Dominick drew their revolvers and it was a standoff. Vito calmly said, "Mr. Walthurs ask your boys to put their guns away so we can continue."

Walthurs quickly said, "Put the guns away boys we'll be fine." Walthurs goons slowly put their guns back in their sport suits.

Vito said, "Phil, Dom, why don't you go out to the bar and show the two boys some card tricks. Maybe they'll get you a cold drink." Vito's men nodded and followed the goons out the door.

Walthurs was visibly nervous. He started to ring his hands and said, "So what's your idea behind this visit?"

Vito tipped his hat a little and said, "Mr. Walthurs I think you're a wise man. I think I'll only need to explain this once. I am a business associate of Don Al Alvano of Waukegan, Illinois. He is a powerful man, you can check it out. Like me he doesn't like violence. He is very concerned for the wellbeing of Tony. If any harm should come to him, you would be the first person he and I would look for. Next would be every living relative of yours. So the consequences to you would be far worse than you losing chump change on the fights. Besides unless you have already kissed and made up with Nicko you still have him to worry about. I will also leave you with another message. The murder of Mel and his army buddy sickens my stomach. So it wouldn't take much to set me off. *Capisce?*"

Walthurs nodded his head and said, "Yes."

Vito took one of Walthurs cigars and lit it. He then placed it between Walthurs lips and said, "Now relax and go on with your life and Tony will go on with his."

After returning to Waukegan Vito revealed everything he had learned of their pa's death to Tony. Tony became furious, "I knew something was wrong. We need to find those ass holes, kick the crap out of them and then whack them."

Vito didn't hesitate. "I swear Tony, if it's the last thing I do, we'll find them and they will pay dearly."

"We are just at the beginning of all this. As we investigate Pa's past, we may learn more that will be disappointing." Vito paused a moment, wanting this to sink in. The end result could involve serious trouble, including a murder conviction that would destroy their lives. "Tony, think this through. If you are to be a part of it I need a total commitment that this will end in the death of the bastards, understanding we may die as well. We have to walk away and live with it with no reservations or feeling of guilt."

Tony looked Vito in the eye and said, "We're brothers and have been through a lot of shit together. It was our pa they killed—we do this together or it doesn't get done. We have no choice. This is our vendetta. The cops have done nothing about it. Now we have to bring justice for our family. There is nothing else for us to understand."

The next morning Tony asked a question of Vito he had wanted to know the answer to for several years. "Vito, what do you do for your business dealings for Alvano? It's no secret you're in his Family, but if you don't want to tell me I'll understand."

Vito answered, "I'm in the idea business. I figure out how the Family can make money and stay away from the Feds. I'm not like Mean Mike. He solves the Don's problems and fixes things."

Tony smiled and said, "That's enough for me Vito. Maybe after we finish our job I can be a guy that fixes things. I'm done with boxing."

"Let's finish our family's business, then we can talk about your future with Alvano. Before that I need to talk to Gwen about our future."

"Is there something wrong between us Vito? I hardly ever see you anymore and when I do you are distant," Gwen said. She had called Vito because it had been two weeks since their last date. She expected more from him at this time of their relationship. Vito said he owed her an apology and an explanation so he arranged to meet Gwen at 6 p.m. at her home and he would take her to a movie and dinner. It would be a special date between the two because he had a surprise for her. Vito recognized long ago how special Gwen was and didn't want to lose her. This was the time he would let her know just how important she was and how much he loved her.

Times were changing and mostly for the worse yet in some regards for the better. Italians were marrying Germans and Protestants were marrying Catholics and many of the unions were successful, and opening the minds of tolerance. Vito knocked on Gwen's front door and was greeted politely by her dad. "May I see Gwen?" asked Vito.

"Of course," responded Gwen's dad.

"Sir, may I speak to you outside first," Vito asked. The two stepped outside and Vito explained what was on his mind: he wanted to marry Gwen. Gwen's Dad explained he was not at all in favor of Vito's profession and it was troublesome to him. It was no secret he was involved with a crime Family and many of their business ventures were immoral. It also troubled him he was Catholic, but his being Italian was not a concern. He had come to know many fine Italians. "I understand," Vito said, "I didn't expect to change your values but I look at it this way--I'm strictly a businessman who works for a Family managed by Al Alvano. I know the consequences of my profession and if Gwen can live with that the rest doesn't matter?" Gwen's dad said he would leave it up to Gwen to decide so long as Vito made it clear what he did for a living. They shook hands. Gwen's dad had agreed to give Gwen's hand to Vito for several reasons; Vito loved Gwen, Gwen loved Vito, Vito was smart and would always be a good provider, and despite his concerns he was also afraid to say no to a person of Vito's status.

Gwen was ready in no time. Before they departed from her house they sat on the front steps. Gwen was nervous and so was Vito. "Gwen I owe you an explanation for my distance and not being around. What I am about to tell you only Tony and only one other knows. I discovered that my pa's car was sabotaged. Someone forced his car off the road and his brake line had been cut and that's why he crashed. I'm trying to figure out who did it and why he was murdered."

"Oh my Vito I am so sorry to hear that. He could be alive today if it were not for that. I know you will not be satisfied till you answer all your questions. You need to be careful," said a tearful Gwen.

"Yes I know. I may be taking a road trip and you may not hear from me for a few days because I'll have to leave without any notice. I also wanted to tell you I am financially secure and what I do for a living should not concern you but I'll explain regardless," Vito said. Vito made it clear he adored her and that he would always be true to her, and further explained his way of making a living, but she should only view it as a way he would provide for her. If she could not accept his way of life he would understand.

Tears came to Gwen's eyes, "I understand. As hard as I think it will be to accept this, it's more important to me that we are together because I love you too." Gwen now knew what Vito did for a living. "You have to promise me you'll stay away from the shooting and killing that we hear about. Just the business deals I know you do already. You need to understand I want us to have a family someday and I want to see you safe in the evenings at home," Gwen said.

"I'm not the violent type and I promise I'll stick to the business deals," Vito said. Vito got on one knee on the porch and proposed to Gwen.

Gwen was as excited as she had ever been in her life and joyously said, "Yes!"

"Great," shouted Vito as he placed an engagement ring on her finger, "we can take care of the particulars later. He took Gwen into his arms and drew her body as close as he could and began a kiss her on her supple lips and moved down her neck. The engagement of their bodies seemed forever which was not long enough. Vito took a deep breath and said, "Let's see if we can find a movie you like and then dinner. Oh by the way I did ask your pa first."

"I wouldn't have expected less," Gwen said.

Once again Vito had disguised himself as a street bum and knocked on Carmine's door. Carmine expected him and opened the door. Carmine said, "I got some interesting news Vito. I know where this Murphy is, but he's not close."

"Where is he that's not close?" Vito asked.

Carmine was outwardly excited and paced back and forth as he talked. "He's supposed to be in Toledo and apparently he's still a fence for small time thieves, you know the B & E kind," reported Carmine. "Here's the other thing. Back in February of 1924 there was a jewelry heist from Bennett's Jewelry store in downtown Toledo. Over a million dollars in jewels and uncut diamonds were stolen; neither the thieves, the diamonds or the jewelry were ever found."

Vito poured himself a shot of Kentucky rye and sat in a stuffed chair thinking of what Carmine had just reported. A few moments later Vito said, "I think I need to take a road trip to Toledo."

"Take me with you. I'll be no trouble and I bet I can help. You don't know how bored I get and I like you and I'd like the suspense."

Vito thought for a moment, finished his Kentucky rye and said, "You're street smart and I think you can help. We leave in two days."

"Good," responded Carmine, "I'll need those days to get off so let me know exactly when we leave."

"Sure thing," Vito said as he handed Carmine $20.

Vito returned to Waukegan and had a lot to think about, including Gwen. He had already decided there would be a vendetta against those responsible for his pa's death, but did he really want to involve Tony or do it on his own? On the other hand it was Tony's pa too and Tony was a big boy now, not just a kid. After all he and his family had been through in life and the heartache. The vendetta was for him and his family and he had no problem with killing those responsible. However, tradition did require he talk to Don Alvano first and get his blessing so long as those he was seeking were not Mafia. From what Vito knew they were not.

CHAPTER 25

The Heist Revealed

Tony had been sitting comfortably reading the Chicago Tribune when he heard. "Tony I want you to grow a beard."

Tony sat up in his chair and looked over the top of his newspaper. "You want me to grow a beard? I thought a mustache was enough for an Italian to be a real man."

"No, that's not why. We're going on a road trip soon and I don't want you recognized. We're going to play the part of small time thieves wanting to make it big time. Then we'll see if we can't get Murphy to bite on something big and from there maybe we can get him to talk. We know Pa wasn't an angel and he could have been involved in that big-time jewelry heist. Carmine "The Weasel" will be traveling with us and he'll see what he can learn on the streets," Vito said.

Tony asked, "I don't know Carmine The Weasel. With a name like that can he be trusted?"

Vito responded, "I'm positive he'll be helpful. He helped finger the goons who nabbed you a few years back. Besides he knows Mean Mike is our cousin and he is terrified of him."

"When do we leave?" Tony asked.

"We'll leave in a couple days, but I need to pay a visit with an old friend of Pa's."

Vito knew his ma would not be working Thursday evening. He also knew Bruno Salvatore was a daily regular at Demark's after working the harbor and Vito would pay him a visit. Vito also brought two of his soldiers along, explaining he would be visiting an acquaintance and he would treat them to whatever they wanted. Bruno was right on time and Vito invited him to his table. "This is unusual Vito. Why would you want to visit with me?" Bruno asked.

Vito wanted to keep their visit to the point. "Bruno you know who I am. I'm not a hit man or a thug. I need to ask you a few questions about my pa. I'll buy you one maybe two beers and by then I want to walk away from here satisfied."

Bruno responded quickly, "Look smart ass I don't scare and you can shove your Family stuff up your ass and the two goons you drug in here too."

"No Bruno, I'm not here to intimidate you. I just need to satisfy my curiosity. You see those two men over there? I wouldn't call them goons they're my body guards and care very much about my feelings." Vito looked over toward a nearby barmaid and raised a hand, "Excuse me Doris," Vito said, "could we have two beers?"

At the thought of a free beer Bruno had calmed down and was quick to add, "Make mine a Pabst."

"Make it two," added Vito.

"Now what's up Vito?" asked Bruno.

"Bruno, you and my pa were friends before he died and now I know his death was no accident. I'm going to find out who killed him and why. I think you know a lot. I also know you were originally from Skokie, moved here, moved away and then came back."

"Ya, so you got a book on me," responded Bruno, "but how do you know your pa's death was no accident?"

Vito said, "Because his car was tampered with--his brake line was cut."

Bruno said, "I always wondered about that too. I didn't kill your pa. I don't know who did for sure, but I could guess. They were after me too."

Vito was surprised, sat straight up in his seat and said, "You're doing good so continue."

Bruno looked toward Vito's soldiers and they smiled. One waved and the other held up a beer. "Your pa and I screwed a big time thug back east.

The night he died I was with him. I have wanted to say something since that night, I couldn't. They think I'm dead too."

Vito's eyebrows raised. He didn't expect to hit the information "Jack Pot" this quick. "Holy shit Bruno. You and my pa must have been in deep."

"We sure as hell were in deep," responded Bruno.

Bruno became silent as Doris returned to their table. "Can I get you guys anything else?" Doris asked.

"Another round of beers here and at the table across from the bar too," requested Vito.

"Sure thing," responded Doris. "How is your little brother doing? I heard he won another big fight."

"He's doing fine, thanks for asking," Vito answered.

Bruno was silent until Doris had moved out of hearing range and then said, "Where was I?"

Vito reminded him, "We were talking about how deep you and my pa were in trouble with the thugs." Vito added, "Bruno, you need to tell me everything. I don't even know what questions to ask. Start with this story you've given me so far."

"How about from the beginning," added Bruno. "First, I was in love with your ma, but your pa and I were *amicos* you know buddies. Sure, at first I was jealous, that is just natural. We were still *amicos*. I'm not justifying anything we did because things are still tough around here for legitimate work and we had to do something better than picking peaches in California or apples in Washington," Bruno said. "Hell it made me sick to hear about those big shots back east and all their railroad money. Your pa and I were between jobs mostly stealing from the rich back east. We knew a fence by the name of Max Murphy. He took most of our loot. Max asks us one day if we want to get in on a heist in Toledo. A really big one, and we asked for more information. Your pa, on the level, was an A-one safe cracker. I could open a house lock, but your pa was special, and they needed him."

"Tell me about the heist," Vito asked.

Bruno took a drink of his beer, "Imagine this Vito. It was supposed to be a job with all of us involved, but your pa and I had to risk the most and do the most. The job was set up by a friend of Murphy's, a big-time crook by the name of Dick Reddick. He was from Cleveland and had a clothing store as a front. Reddick said he had inside word from a day guard who used to work for him and was at the time working for Bennett Jewelry. He knew they would have a shipment of uncut diamonds delivered in a month." Bruno took a sip of his beer and lit a cigarette then looked around the room to assure himself no one else was listening. "We both knew Murphy from some previous deals. He called us in and he was dependable to get us the best buck for our merchandise. I asked your pa if he wanted to get involved and your pa asked. 'What's in it for us? If we have to crack a safe we get 60% of the take.' I agreed. Just because they give us information isn't enough. Murphy said Reddick had a vacant shop rented right next to Bennett's. The buildings share walls like row homes." Bruno continued to tell the story as if he was in a trance.

CHAPTER 26

The Bennett Jewelry Heist

"Three days after the meeting with Murphy Angelo and I were in Toledo and we checked into the Riverside Hotel. Then we drove to Bennett's Jewelry to case the place."

"Excuse me," said Angelo to a clerk, "could I have this watch appraised? I bought it two years ago and I don't think these are real diamonds."

"Of course," said the clerk, "wait just a moment." Angelo and Bruno calculated the store's layout, making a mental map: the main office, jeweler's work area, the safe location although it could barely be seen. The store even had a public rest room. The viewing cases were loaded with exceptionally fine arrangements of jewelry: watches, pins, broaches, necklaces, rings, and pendants. It was an extraordinary jewelry store; there wasn't anything they didn't have.

Angelo looked at Bruno, smiled and said, "Wonderful shop."

"Sir, we estimate your watch to have a value of about $100, and they are diamonds indeed, but not high quality. We could improve the value with better cut stones," reported the clerk.

"No, that's fine, you've been a big help," answered Angelo. The two walked out the door toward Angelo's car. After they started to drive off

Angelo said, "Did you notice the place had a dual alarm system including the Holmes type that works off a phone line?"

Bruno was surprised. "No, that must mean we have to cut the electric and the phone line to disable the alarm systems. So we're in this deal?"

Angelo came back, "Yup, we'll get in and make a killing, those chumps aren't going to take us for saps."

Angelo and Bruno checked back into the same hotel a week later and had a business talk at the Big House Lounge, in Toledo, with Reddick, and the fence Murphy. "It's like this," explained Reddick, "I got this shop rented, under a fictitious name of course, right next to Bennett's. At night we break through a common wall and in we go." Angelo asked how long he had it rented for and Reddick said he had a year lease and had paid one month's rent. Reddick continued, "I understand you already cased the place, so I'll have a driver ready with a car in the back. I'll watch the street from the front window. You two open the safe and the show cases."

"Sounds good. What's our cut?" Angelo asked.

"You guys get 30 percent," responded Reddick.

Bruno said, "That isn't Jack Shit, the two of you get 70%! You need us to get into the damn safe."

"Look I ain't here to haggle and I got all the info. You two in or not?" asked Reddick.

Angelo quickly said, "We're in."

A Duncan's armored truck pulled up to Bennett's Jewelry two weeks later. Two armed guards got out and opened a locked back door. The day guard of Bennett's held open the store door while one armed guard carried the merchandise in and the second stood watch. That night the day guard was alleged to have passed word to Reddick the diamonds had been delivered. Within two days an entry hole was opened with only the jewelry store's thin wood wall intact. That Saturday night Angelo, Bruno, Reddick and his driver were set for the heist. At 2:30 a.m. Bruno cut the electric and phone lines from a common power pole at the rear of the two buildings. At 2:35 a.m. the wall was broken out and the three entered Bennett's. Angelo and Bruno had been told a car would be waiting down the alley. Angelo was smiling and said, "For such a big store this is an old Hall's floor safe. I can't believe it. I'll have this open quick." Angelo got out a few tools including a stethoscope and within a few minutes he had the safe open and placed the contents into a carpet bag. Bruno was grabbing jewelry from the show cases as fast as he could when he noticed the more expensive jewels were gone.

"Crap," Bruno shouted, "there has to be another safe. Angelo, Angelo the best stuff isn't here."

"I got the diamonds, but damn it you're right," Angelo said as he flashed a dim light across the remaining show cases. "We need to search for a hidden safe."

"Hurry up you guys," yelled Reddick, "a car is coming, put out the light. Damn, it's a cop car," shouted Reddick. "Heads down! Oh, my. It's a taxi we're okay."

Angelo and Bruno took deep breaths just to calm down. "Most of the time these double safe situations have a wall safe covered by something like a picture," Angelo said as he walked to a picture of the jewelry store's founder. Angelo moved the picture to the side, there was nothing behind it.

"Oh my God! Is this the owner's wife? She is as ugly as the butt end of one of those nasty red-assed zoo monkeys," commented Bruno. He pushed the picture aside to discover a small wall safe. "Here we go," whispered Bruno. Angelo moved immediately to it and on his second try opened it and found the remaining jewelry.

Reddick turned and asked Angelo and Bruno for the carpet bag. They refused to hand it to him. A search light from a squad car came through the large store window and caught the back of Riddick's head. Within seconds a siren was sounding and the police were at the door. The three scrambled for the hole in the wall, and the police broke in. Two late shots were fired at the hole as the bandits ran out the back with Bruno in the lead and Angelo following, as they passed out the door they ran to their left. Reddick ran right and down the alley to a waiting car. There was a third shot fired by a cop just as Reddick turned to look. He returned fire, killing one cop in the alley. Reddick opened the passenger door and jumped in. "Where the hell are the two *Goombahs*," the driver shouted.

"They ran the wrong way and they got the loot," yelled Reddick.

By the time Bruno and Angelo discovered the getaway car was in the opposite direction, it was too late for them to turn around. They escaped in an unplanned frenzy. The two hid behind trash cans. Then a car quickly approached them from the opposite end of the alley. "Here they come," whispered Bruno as he started to rise.

"Stop, wait," whispered an excited Angelo. "That may not be Reddick." It wasn't Reddick--it was a cop car. After the cop car slowly drove by Angelo whispered. "That was too close. Why the hell did we run the wrong direction? We gotta get out of here!" The two had no clue what direction to go with the entire night's take worth perhaps a million dollars. As soon as the cop car stopped in the alley and turned down a main street, Bruno and Angelo ran between two buildings to a side street. They continued running, slowing and hiding only when a car came by, until they reached a main thoroughfare. "We need to get back to the hotel and get the hell out of here," Angelo said.

"Right! We need to keep going till we spot a taxi," Bruno agreed.

After an hour the two flagged down a cab. "Where to boys?" asked a curious cabby.

"Take us to the Riverside Hotel," Angelo said.

"Say you guys hear about the robbery and cop murder tonight?" asked the cabby.

"No, we were drinking most of the night and hadn't heard," Bruno said.

The cabby then added, "Yup! A big jewelry store was robbed and a cop was killed. You always carry a big carpet bag like that when you're drinking?"

"Shut up," shouted Bruno. "Just get us to the Riverside."

"Just clowning," said the cabby. Within 20 minutes the cabby had the two to their hotel. "A buck twenty five, boys," the cabby said. Bruno paid him and the two took off for their room.

Angelo and Bruno entered their room. "We need to get the hell out of here and now," Angelo said. "That cabby will rat on us quick." They packed their bags and slipped out a back door. They hustled for Angelo's car and within minutes they were headed west to Kenosha. Within five minutes the cabby had reported his encounter with Bruno and Angelo and the carpet bag to the cops. Five minutes after Bruno and Angelo left their room the cops were at the hotel.

It took over a day before Bruno and Angelo got back to Kenosha and Bruno's apartment.

"Murphy, where the hell did your *Goombah* buddies go?" asked Riddick.

"I sure as hell don't know," answered Murphy. "Weren't you supposed to bring them back with you?"

"Ya, I forgot to tell them where the car would be and they ran the wrong way, now they're gone. They got the night's take and I don't even know what we got." Riddick said. "I'm pissed--they should have come back here by now."

"From what you said they are likely out of here. If that's the case I know how to get in touch with them," Murphy said.

"I'm okay with that so long as they don't pull a fast one on us," Reddick said. After a few days Murphy called Bruno and made arrangements to meet him at his place on Clark Street in Chicago.

"Bruno, I say we high-grade this job and then make a second split with them. I'm keeping this cute bow for Maria," Angelo said.

Bruno agreed. "I'm fine with that. Did you see the news? Those jack asses left us for dead and killed a cop. The cabby reported us and is some kind of hero now. The cops accused us of the cop's murder too."

"Damn, we didn't even have a piece. I'm no choir boy, but I'd sooner be caught for B and E than whacking a cop," Angelo said.

Bruno paused a moment. "Well, Riddick and Murphy don't know what we took and they won't trust us either. We can't hide forever, so we need to meet and split the take after we high grade. So be prepared for the worst."

Bruno caught himself and looked at Vito as if to awaken from being hypnotized. He took a long gulp of beer and continued. "Vito, Murphy assured us we would be safe so this was the plan: we met with the three of them including the driver. His name was Bruce something I can't remember. We brought the carpet bag up after we took some of the jewels, but kept about 40% of the diamonds, so everything we had left over we would split. They must have known we stiffed them. I guess we were the fools because things went to hell real quick in Murphy's place. We left before things got too out of hand." Bruno finished his beer and said, "As we drove off a large delivery truck side-swiped us. I didn't understand what was happening at fist. On the second swipe the truck forced us off the road and down the bank of the Chicago River. Angelo kept pushing his brake pedal and said there was something wrong. Your pa shouted, 'No brakes, they're gone.' We rolled downhill and the car struck a tree and we went into the river. I kept shouting, 'Angelo, Angelo get out, get out!' The brakes must have been messed with. When they found your pa's body and not mine they assumed I was swept down the river and I was, a little ways. I broke my arm and cracked some ribs and crawled to shore about a half a block away. After that I laid low in North Carolina with friends and then came back here after I heard Riddick and Murphy had moved."

Vito was astounded. He had learned more in the last few minutes than he ever expected. The accident was about as Eric described it. Bruno explained, "My best bet would be Murphy set up our meeting for us to get whacked. I don't know for certain because I didn't hear anything. Reddick and this Bruce were responsible too."

Vito took a swig of his beer and commented, "This Milwaukee beer is okay, but when those old German Brewmiester's worked for Capone I think they did a better job."

"Are you serious Vito?" exclaimed Bruno. "After all I told you, you think of beer?"

"No Bruno, I am overwhelmed, you have told me so much more than I expected that I need to figure some things out. I believe you, and I just need to figure out how to get the finger on the right guys. Next time tell me what happened in Murphy's. I really want to know, but right now it is hard for me to imagine my pa was a thief after all."

"Vito, next time I'll tell you the story of what happened inside, but when you decide what to do let me in. I need some piece of mind. Besides there's still a couple hundred G's worth of loot your pa stashed somewhere." Bruno had fenced his portion and despite being set for life continued working to offset any suspicion. The fact Vito's pa had hidden a large portion of his jewels and diamonds didn't go unnoticed.

"Okay Bruno, have another beer on me. When the time comes I'll call on you." Vito laid two bucks down on the table, sat with his body guards a few minutes and started to leave Demark's when he turned and walked back to Bruno. In a low voice he said, "So the rumors about my pa and the heist were true. I knew looking into his past would bring out some disappointment. But then look at me."

CHAPTER 27

The Search for Murphy

"Nice beard Tony," Vito said with a smile.

Tony responded with a grin, "Not bad is it? I look 20 years older."

Vito then became serious, "We'll be heading to Toledo soon." Vito had accumulated about two grand's worth of jewelry and watches from pawn shops and an estate sale, enough to maybe convince Murphy they were genuine thieves. Two days later Vito, Big Tony and Carmine were in Toledo and checked into a cheap hotel. Toledo wasn't nearly as big as Chicago.

"We fit right in guys," Carmine said. "I'll learn what I can tomorrow and see you back here at the hotel at 10 p.m." The next day Tony and Vito set out to find where Murphy lived and follow him around. The brothers struck out the first day. Murphy wasn't in any of the phone books and the operator had numerous Murphy's.

The brothers decided to check out the scene of the crime and to their surprise there was no jewelry store. Instead there was a furniture store in a relatively new building, not the pre-1900s building they expected. The manager of the furniture store explained that after the robbery in 1924 there was a second robbery a year later during which the old building was burned and the charred remains of Bennett Sr. were found. It was rumored that Bennett Jr. had collected insurance on both robberies and the building, which seemed peculiar. Meanwhile Carmine had done well. He learned that Murphy hung out at a cheap bar on the south side of Toledo called the Big House Lounge.

The Big House Lounge was located in a sleazy part of Toledo and the neighborhood next to it was more or less a ghetto. Vito decided to park in a lot across the street belonging to a lounge, the Emerald Island. After parking, the three got out of their car and heard a voice. "You Crackers took my favorite spot." Vito turned and saw three colored men stood nearby, two with knives.

"We won't be long," Vito said not wanting to back down.

"The shit you say, you moving now," one of the men said. Before long a crowd had gathered.

Then a fourth colored man came forward and said, "Winston, back off man, look across yonder." Across the street on the sidewalk of the Big House Lounge were seven Wise Guys. They unbuttoned their sport coats in unison and the crowd dispersed back into the Emerald Island.

"It may be a good time to move your car," Carmine said. Vito agreed, saying that the spaces were larger across the street, anyway.

After moving the car, Vito, Tony and Carmine stepped into the Big House Lounge only to find themselves an attraction. One of the Wise Guys commented they would have been Swiss cheese if someone hadn't seen what was going on. Vito thanked the fellas who stepped outside on their behalf, explaining all they wanted for the evening was a cold beer and maybe a dance or two. A second Wise Guy said, "You won't get a dance from me, pal."

Vito, Tony and Carmine took on new names as they casually mingled with the crowd. Carmine approached a drunk from the streets and started small talk about unloading some low grade stuff of his ex-wife's. "You want Murphy," the drunk whispered.

"Murphy isn't here," said an eavesdropping older man. "He usually comes in around 10."

Vito responded, "We've never met him and we wouldn't recognize him unless someone introduced him to us."

"He's hard to miss. He dresses like a pimp and has sideburns that slide down under his chin," explained the eavesdropper. He then looked down on the floor and saw a partially spent cigarette and picked it up. "Looky, looky here," he said, "this is my lucky night."

After a few beers the three were enjoying the evening when Tony spotted Murphy. "Vito, look over there: that old guy didn't tell us much, but that must be him."

"Sure it is," said Carmine. "He's dressed in broads, they're hanging all over him."

"Let's let him get settled in and Carmine you talk to him first," directed Vito.

Twenty minutes went by before Carmine got up from his table and introduced himself to Murphy. Carmine was surprised when Murphy said, "So what can I do for you or are you a damn cop or just an old has been cop?"

"No," responded Carmine, "I need some help."

"Keep going," Murphy said.

Carmine pretended to be nervous. "I've got two grand of my ex-wife's jewels I need to unload and that old guy over there said you could help."

Murphy responded, "Are you shitting me? You want me to fence two Gs of merchandise you stole from your ex? That's not my business!"

Vito stepped over to the table. "Sir, please excuse my pa. He isn't all here and sometimes he gets carried away. Can I further my apology by buying you and your lady friends a drink?"

Murphy started to laugh and thought a drink would be fine. "Say young fella, who are you?"

Vito smiled, "My name's Vincent Sorrento, my dad Richard, and my brother is over at the corner table, his name's Joe."

"So where are you boys from?" Murphy asked.

"Right now, here, I suppose. We came east to find work," Vito paused and continued. "We're not broke, we just need to find some work, any work. We're staying at a local hotel while we have a few bucks." Vito did not want to give the impression they were desperate and added that they just needed a break. Vito said, "Please excuse us." The two joined Tony and enjoyed the night. They planned to return to the lounge after they went back to Waukegan.

Vito opened a letter addressed to a bogus company. The letter read, "Dear Proprietor of the Ames Petroleum Company. It has come to our attention that you are now delinquent on the transfer of state gasoline sales tax to the Honorable Treasurer Gene Williams. It's estimated that the total is $33,222 over the past two years. Please immediately transfer to the State of Wisconsin account this total. Also be advised this is our third and final request and if we do not receive these funds within five working days we will take legal action." Vito then called one of his body guards. "Dom, will you please close the Ames Petroleum Company postal box in Racine and open a new one in Burlington under Quality Petroleum Products!"

Dom answered immediately, "Consider it done Vito." Vito expected a few more similar letters to arrive and the result would be the same: he would close a postal box in one city and open a new one in another. Vito had also delivered 65 more pinball machines to bowling alleys and dance halls throughout a tri-state area. He could hardly keep up with the demand, especially since there was no competition.

Kaiser and Enrico stepped into Vito's office without knocking which startled him. Vito jumped at the sound of the door opening. "Holy shit guys, lucky I didn't have a piece in my hand or I would have blown someone's nuts off."

Kaiser looked at Enrico and said, "I should have known better. The cool Vito Cosenza must have his mind on a few more things than just making money and keeping the Don happy. I bet he was thinking of that cute girl friend of his."

"So what are you up to Vito?" asked Enrico.

"Just business, guys, just business! So what's up with you two?" asked Vito.

Kaiser said, "Let's go talk to the Don. I think he has some travel plans for you. But finish what you're doing and next time we'll knock." Vito knew better than to keep the Don waiting and walked across the compound with his two companions.

After being recognized by one of the soldiers all three walked into the Don's office. Alvano set his cigar in an ashtray and offered one to his associates. Alvano started the conversation. "Vito, I think everyone in the Family understand how well you have done for us these past two years."

Vito said, "I enjoy working for the Family, and I'm pleased to be of service. I make a good living and I'm glad you're happy."

The Don continued, "Vito once you told me every Italian boy wanted one of three businesses in his life: a strip lounge, an Italian restaurant, or an olive oil company. Kaiser and I decided that we would try our hand at olive oil since we have the other two already."

Vito needed a mental break. "When do we leave and where are we headed?"

Kaiser jumped in, "We leave in three weeks and it may take a week at sea. We'll travel to the village of Alcarmo, Sicily." Vito realized he had to act soon to avenge his pa's death.

CHAPTER 28

The Vendetta

Vito and Bruno met one more time at Demark's before they would return to Toledo. Bruno still hadn't finished describing what had happened in Murphy's apartment on Clark Street. Bruno had arrived early for their meeting so to pass the time he flipped a coin. Heads, heads, tales and he wondered for a moment if his life was like the toss of a coin: would it have had more fulfillment if Maria had fallen for him and not Angelo?

"Bruno, I'm here," Vito said with enthusiasm. Vito sat down and asked Bruno to finish his story.

Bruno looked up at Vito and gathered his wits then explained, "Murphy contacted us to set up a meeting with everyone involved and we met at his place. Angelo and I high graded the loot beforehand and placed the remainder in the same carpet bag used in the heist. We brought only what we would divide up with them. The meeting seemed to go well at first, but as I said earlier it went to hell. We thought we had settled on how the loot would be split up and the meeting was finished. At first they seemed satisfied and believed we showed them everything. Then Riddick became suspicious and demanded to see what else was in the bag. When I told them there was nothing else in the bag, they were irritated beyond belief. Riddick's expected share of the jewels and uncut diamonds was far less than what we gave him. He wanted 500 Gs. So I pulled out my piece and threatened to blow the two of them away. Angelo gave them hell too because we got labeled cop killers. The cabby gave the cops a description of us. The cops didn't even know about Riddick and his driver. When we left they were pissed and thought they'd never see us again. I think Riddick and Murphy thought we had all the loot with us in the bag, hard to say. I think their plan all along was to rub us out and grab the bag with all the loot. It wasn't in the bag and after the crash the bag wasn't in the car—otherwise the cops would have had some suspicions. I had the bag and it had very little in it because of the split with them and the rest was in Kenosha. So I had part of your pa's share."

Bruno knew where his share was, but he didn't know where the rest of Angelo's was. Vito asked Bruno, "What do you suppose happened to the jewels and diamonds my pa had? I know my ma wouldn't know. She doesn't have any idea he was a crook. That only means the loot has to be around somewhere in or near the Pontillos' home or our old apartment."

Bruno folded his arms and said, "At the end I was getting worried. Your pa was getting soft and talked about going straight. He also talked about Confession with Father Falbo. Your pa was far more religious than I ever was. So I think he wouldn't have felt right until he said something to Father Falbo. But I don't get it, what would that really accomplish?"

Vito shook his head side to side and said, "Did he go to Confession after your discussion? I know he really liked Father Falbo."

Bruno took a long gulp of beer, wiped his face, "He never mentioned it again." The big question remained unanswered. Where was Angelo's loot?

Bruno wanted to make sure where he stood with the Cosenza brothers and said, "Vito, I want you to understand you and your brother are good kids, but I still think of you as kids. Don't take offense--I do respect both of you. We're not *amicos*."

Vito said, "Ya, I never thought different. We have a common vengeance. To you it is survival and to us it's family justice. When we are done, nothing is said of the vendetta. We go our own way. Regardless I'm glad we had a chance to talk because I understand you now. Don't take this as an offense, I always thought of you as a big blow hard."

Bruno gave a halfhearted smile and said, "Now listen to me some more, and don't take offense." Bruno explained he thought Vito was trying too hard with his cat and mouse game he had planned. He had a simpler plan. The outcome for the goons would be the same. They would go after

Murphy first, push him into telling them where the other two jerks were and then whack him and go after Reddick and his driver Bruce. Bruno asked, "Do you really understand the business you're in? Who you really are? You're as much a thug as Alvano's Wise Guys. You're trying too hard to be a choir boy at the same time. Vito, you're as much a criminal as they are. Just because you justify your work for Alvano as a business doesn't mean you're not a criminal!"

Vito thought for a few moments, looked at his glass of beer and said, "I know you're right. I have been kidding myself about the violence and fraud, but I'm not going to make this some kind of a confessional. I like what I do and I'm good at it. Now we have this vendetta, we are set to take three lives for my family's justice and society will view it as criminal. You're right again that the outcome is the same. We slip into Murphy's place and wait for him, get our information and whack him like a fly then go after the others. It's simple."

Bruno was relieved that Vito saw it like it really was. "When we locate Murphy's home, I'll get us in," he said.

Vito, Tony and Bruno returned to Toledo and checked into a local hotel providing false names again. Vito and Tony revisited the Big House Lounge several nights in a row before Murphy finally showed up. At the end of the evening Murphy left with one of his girlfriends and the Cosenza brothers followed them to what they believed was his girlfriend's apartment. They waited in their car until nearly daylight before Murphy left her apartment and went home. The following night the three waited in their car near Murphy's home. The trio waited till dark then walked through an alley to Murphy's back door. Bruno had no problem picking the skeleton key lock. The plan was set and now they only had to wait.

About 2 a.m. Murphy returned home, turned his living room light on and saw Bruno sitting on his couch. Murphy was startled and shouted, "Oh my God."

Bruno smiled and said, "Why Murphy, you act like you've seen a ghost."

Murphy blurted out, "You're supposed to be dead!"

Bruno smiled, "No Murphy I'm not dead. I'd like to introduce you to Angelo's two boys, Vito and Tony. They have been waiting a long time to meet you."

Vito and Tony stepped out from the shadows. "Have a seat," ordered Vito. Murphy quickly began to stutter and looked toward Vito and Tony and then Bruno. His anxiety level was elevated to the highest level he could have imagined. He knew the brothers had one thing in mind—a vendetta.

Murphy nervously said, "Okay so you're alive. Look kid it wasn't my idea to kill your dad and Bruno, on the level, it was Reddick and Bennett's. Don't you see? Why would I have them whacked? I made a living off fencing their stuff. I argued against it, but Riddick said no and Swenson cut the brake lines."

"Who the hell is Swenson?" barked Bruno. "And what does Bennett have to do with it? We robbed him!"

"We make a deal first. I know what you want to do to me. Let me go and I'll never say a word. Because if I do talk, I implicate myself," pleaded Murphy. Vito looked at Bruno and he nodded his head just as he was giving Murphy a pencil and paper. Murphy started talking and the more he talked the more interesting it got. Bennett Jr. was as evil as the year was long. The way he figured it Bennett Jr. was in gambling debt and couldn't get a loan from his dad. So Bennett arranged through underworld connections to have their jewelry store robbed by Riddick and Swenson. His dad was so tight Bennett Jr. didn't know the combination to the safe and didn't even know about the wall safe. It was insulting to him and he hated his dad. So they needed an ace safe cracker like Angelo. I told them how good Angelo was. Swenson was just a chump off the street who knew something about cars.

Bennett was to get the cash from the majority of the take and collect insurance. In the end Bennett and Riddick decided to whack everyone involved, except Murphy, to have a bigger take. Murphy explained he wasn't sure about what happened with the second robbery and the fire or the death of Bennett Sr.

Vito stared at Murphy as he thought the story through then turned to the window and looked through the blinds. He thought so this is Murphy, a simple yet shrewd man. He poured himself a shot of Murphy's cheap whiskey and said, "He's telling the truth. Tony and I talked to the manager of a furniture store built after the fire. He said that Bennett Jr. had collected on insurance several times, on the jewelry and the building."

"Now I get it," Bruno said, "Bennett was the one who told Riddick when the diamonds were delivered, not a guard."

"That's right," Murphy said. "It was a hoax, no guard was involved."

"So where are Reddick, Bruce and Swenson now?" asked Vito. Murphy began to laugh, which surprised the three, and then Murphy explained Swenson was dead, as was Bruce: the driver of their get-away car. Riddick and Bennett had them whacked shortly after Angelo was killed. Murphy was like a wind up doll and wouldn't shut up, offering information they didn't even ask for. Murphy said Riddick lived just outside Cleveland in Ogden, Ohio.

Just as Murphy completed his ratting, Bruno was about to smash Murphy's neck with a tire iron when Vito yelled, "Stop, what about Bennett?"

Murphy jumped instinctively when he saw the tire iron poised over his head and quickly said, "Bennett, I don't know where he is for sure other than according to Riddick his wife left him last year and he lives near Cleveland. Bennett moved after the fire. I'll draw you a map of how to find Riddick's." Then he looked to Vito and said, "If you don't whack him he will whack me for sure so do the job." Murphy was visibly shaken when he saw Bruno still holding the tire iron.

Vito said, "Okay Murphy, I think you'll keep your mouth shut just as you did for Bennett." Vito, Tony and Bruno left Murphy to himself and set out for Cleveland to find Riddick and Bennett.

The vendetta trio returned to their hotel room and discussed what they had learned and what the next step would be. It all made sense now to Vito and he said, "Bennett must have killed his own dad, robbed the place himself, and then set fire to the building to destroy any evidence. What he may not have planned on was burning most of the block with his jewelry store. He is as evil as they come."

Next was the decision of what plan to proceed with. They had numerous strategies, but Tony's idea was the best. "If we can get Bennett and Riddick in the same place it will simplify everything. Think of this," Tony explained. "We check out Bennett's and Riddick's place and whoever has the most secluded we meet him first and then invite the second for a visit." Vito and Bruno liked the concept.

The following morning the three set out to case Riddick's place first. It was a modest bungalow surrounded with neighbors, yet no visible security. Bennett's place was outside Cleveland, isolated, with a manual security gate. He had a beautiful home with a huge manicured yard. "We got the perfect place to grab both guys," Tony said. Vito and Bruno agreed. The plan was set.

Night couldn't come soon enough. Bruno slipped under several bushes marking Bennett's property line and picked the back door lock while Bennett was in his living room reading a paper. Tony opened Bennett's gate and the two drove up with the car lights off. They quietly left their car and rang Bennett's doorbell. As Bennett turned his porch light on and checked through a security peep in the door, Bruno slipped up behind him. To Bruno's surprise Bennett who had been living on pins and needles panicked when he saw two unfamiliar faces and turned to run. In an instant he saw Bruno and shoved him to the side and ran out the back door. Vito could see through the corner of a curtain and said, "He's running to the back." Tony ran to the back of the house to catch Bennett. Vito shouted, "No Tony, no, he may have a gun." Tony disregarded Vito's yelling and ran him down. Tony tackled Bennett, shoved his face in the thick grass and put him in a vicious neck lock, choking him unconscious. Bruno then held the back door open and Tony entered dragging a limp Bennett. Vito drove across Bennett's lawn and parked their car on the side.

"Does this guy stink of booze or what?" Bruno said. "He must have a bottle somewhere he'd like to share with us."

When Bennett woke he was tied to a kitchen chair. Bennett looked at the trio and asked, "Who the hell are you guys?"

Vito answered, "Well, we're from an insurance company and we're thinking of raising premiums for a jewelry store."

"Bullshit," shouted Bennett, "you want some kind of a ransom?"

"No, but maybe I should teach you some manners," Bruno said.

"So who are you?" Bennett asked again.

"We'll get to that," Vito said. "First we need some answers to a few questions. Tell us about the heist in 1924."

"You'll find all you need to know in the papers," answered Bennett.

Bruno took a huge gulp of Bennett's open bottle of whiskey then he and Vito started getting rough with him, but to no avail. Until Bruno smashed one of Bennett's fingers with a nut cracker and then threatened to smash his knees with a tire iron. Bennett started chattering like a chipmunk, saying his dad was a tight ass and had no respect for him. When Bennett told his dad he was in financial trouble his dad only laughed. Bennett thought he would have enough money with his first conspiracy to have the jewelry store robbed and then collect on the insurance, but that two of the criminals involved took off with more than their share. Both were supposed to have been killed, but he never got his full share of the loot.

After Bennett finished they had him call Riddick and say he needed to come quick for some new developments. Riddick first asked Bennett if he had been drinking again. Then said he had a date, but would cancel if it meant money in his pocket. Riddick had an hour drive so it left plenty of time for more dialogue with Bennett. After the call, Bennett explained he thought he was able to siphon some of the insurance money off the store. It took a year to come and his dad counted every penny of it. His dad discovered a lot of it was missing. Bennett said he and his dad argued and that his dad was in a rage during the argument. He said his dad accused him of stealing from the business and started shoving him and that is when he struck his dad, who fell and cracked his head on the floor. Bennett claimed it was an accident. To cover his dad's death he decided to steal the stores jewels and was lucky the main vault was unlocked. He then set the store on fire and slipped out the back unnoticed. Bennett said, "Let me go and you'll all get 50Gs each."

"Wow," said Bruno, "You'll pay us all that? Oh by the way my name is Bruno Salvatore and this is Tony and Vito Cosenza--you had their pa killed."

"Salvatore, I thought you were dead along with that cheap ass Cosenza," blurted Bennett. Just as he finished talking Tony broke Bennett's jaw with a powerful roundhouse right that rendered Bennett unconscious again.

"Man you have a violent brother Vito!" Bruno said. "He needs counseling."

"I didn't like what he said about Pa," Tony said.

An hour passed and Tony's stomach grumbled. "Vito, I'm hungry, I'm going to check this chump's ice box and see if he has some salami or cheese." Tony went to Bennett's kitchen and started exploring his cupboards and found a new refrigerator.

Riddick was suspicious of the phone call he had received from Bennett. He decided not to take the chance of just knocking on his door. Riddick parked his car well away from Bennett's home and saw that the gate was open, something Bennett never allowed. Riddick crept in the dark low to the ground with his piece drawn. The night was very dark and to his advantage. Riddick was startled when a neighbor's dog began barking. Riddick became motionless and laid down in the grass. The barking ceased when its master called him into his house. Then Riddick noticed Vito's car parked on the grass. He peered through a slight opening of a drawn curtain, he could barely see a tied and gagged Bennett and two goons sitting in nearby chairs. He could hear talking and soon was aware he recognized one of the goons. He slipped around to the back of the house and found an unlocked door. Riddick opened it slowly and silently slipped in. Cautiously he moved to the front where Bennett was tied up and Vito and Bruno were sitting comfortably. Riddick stepped into the same room as Vito and Bruno, catching them off guard. He held them at bay with his piece. "So, Bruno you're alive. I was afraid of that. Who is your young chum, your kid?" Bennett was extremely animated trying to warn Riddick of Tony in the kitchen, but Riddick ignored his motion and speech impediment. "I hope you have lived a good life at our expense you asshole. The only mistake we made was not whacking Murphy too," growled Riddick. Oh by the way the cops are still looking for a cop killer who robbed Bennett's jewelry ten years ago

"Sure we did," said Bruno. "I also spent a few years on the lam because we got the blame for the cop's murder"

Tony had a mouth full of provolone cheese when he heard an unfamiliar voice from the living room. He quietly picked up a long-necked wine bottle and walked carefully toward the unfamiliar voice. Bennett continued with his motions and with his broken jaw was muttering just as Riddick turned to untie Bennett's gag, Tony clubbed him with the wine bottle. Riddick fell to the floor unconscious.

"I just wasted a good bottle of *vino*," complained Tony.

Riddick was tied and gagged and as he came to he saw Tony. Tony glared at him and said, "You piece of shit you two had my pa killed and now I'm going to tell you how you'll die. We'll roll you up in a rug like a hot dog and take you out on a big lake. Then wrap a chain around the rug and over you go. There'll be nothing you can do as the water rolls in you'll kick and try to catch your last breath. You'll feel your body sinking. Your lungs will fill with water, you'll gasp and it will be over."

The long drive back to Kenosha harbor was quiet other than the road noise and an occasional thump in the trunk. Vito kept thinking of what his life would have been like if his pa had a legitimate job and he grew up with a mentor. His nanu had been good to him as had his uncles, but it wasn't like having a real pa to talk to about life. He also thought about Tony and if he had done right by him while he was growing up and what was in his future. Would allowing him to work for the Alvano Family be the right thing to do now that he was through with boxing, or would he be better off trying to find a job in a jobless world? Vito wondered where Angelo's loot was and if he ever gave a Confession? Now he wondered about Father Falbo, and how could a priest afford the kind of car he owned?

A light drizzle started adding an eerie ambience to the last few miles of the trip. Bruno was driving when he spoke, "Another 15 miles and we'll be to the harbor about 2 a.m. I'll grab one of our work boats. Nobody will know the difference."

The light drizzle had continued and it slid into Vito's eyes. He blinked as he looked at the two rolled rugs lying at the bottom of the large wooden work boat Bruno had commandeered. There was time to change his mind, to forgive, forget, and release them. No--Reddick and Bennett had made their mistake over a decade earlier to work it out with his pa and Bruno, they didn't. After his pa's murder there was no investigation. This was Vito's family justice. Vito, Tony and his family had suffered too long without a parent, husband, son-in-law and a brother-in-law. He had already decided they would die for their thoughtless killing. Vito looked at Tony and said, "Tony you don't have to help. We can handle this."

"No, they killed a part of me too. When they die I get satisfaction in my life too knowing this is our justice. Nobody knows a thing and I'll no longer be troubled with why nothing was ever done." Tony put his hands on his hips and then folded his arms on his chest and said, "Pa was a criminal, but he didn't deserve to die at the hands of these greedy bastards."

Bruno interrupted and said, "Now it will end. All my years of looking behind my back are over." Bruno slowed the boat down when he could barely see the lights off Kenosha. Then one after the other the rugs slid into the water with only the noise of the tow chain slipping over the wooden gunwale and the loud slush of the rug hitting the water. A few bubbles rose to the surface. The deed was done and the vendetta complete.

Other than the noise of the diesel engine all was silent during the return to shore until Vito said, "Tony I need to ask once more. Do you feel guilty? I don't. I feel nothing, no joy or excitement, we are done. Our vendetta is finished!"

"No I don't feel any guilt, but I still don't understand the meaning of life. Maybe I never will."

Vito had to have conversation with Father Falbo. He knew Father Falbo had to know something about his pa's criminal deeds. So Saturday evening he walked with his family to Holy Sacrament for Confession. In Vito's mind he would be the only one of the Cosenza brothers to burn in Hell; the sin was his alone. Vito also understood that in order to receive God's Grace of forgiveness one must be truly sorry. He was sorry he had to commit the sin, but he was not sorry for serving justice. When his turn came he walked to the Confessional. "Forgive me Father for I have sinned, my last Confession was two months ago."

Father Falbo replied, "Yes my Son God bless you, continue."

"Father I fulfilled my vendetta. I set out to terminate the men who murdered my pa and I think I have one more man to find to answer a lingering question about my pa." Father Falbo paused a few moments and became nervous. It brought back more memories from a Confession he had with Angelo over a decade earlier. Father Falbo had made a promise he did not keep and now it was haunting him. He knew the jewels were hidden in the statue of the St Mary in the Pontillos' home. What should he do? He knew he had to think it all through and come to the right decision.

Father Falbo said, "My Son the vendetta of which you speak may be an offense of God's Commandment—Thou Shalt Not Kill. Where are these men now?"

"Father they sleep with the fishes."

The End of Part I